"Do I look like someone who cares what God thinks?"
PINHEAD

Also by Peter Atkins

Novels
Morningstar (1992)

Big Thunder (1997)

Moontown (2008)

Collections
Wishmaster & Other Stories (1999)

Spook City (2009)
with Clive Barker and Ramsey Campbell

Rumours of the Marvellous (2011)

Cemetery Dance Select: Peter Atkins (2015)

All Our Hearts Are Ghosts (Forthcoming)

Screenplays
Hellbound: Hellraiser II (1988)

Hellraiser III: Hell on Earth (1992)

Fist of the North Star (1995)

Hellraiser: Bloodline (1996)

Wishmaster (1997)

Prisoners of the Sun (2013)

THE ORIGINAL SCREENPLAY

Peter Atkins

The motion picture
Hellraiser:Bloodline copyright © Miramax, LLC 1996

Publication rights to this screenplay
copyright © Peter Atkins, per WGA
separation of rights agreement

All Rights Reserved.

Cover Image - Pinhead 30th anniversary re-design
by Cris Alex and Stephen Imhoff Jr.

The characters and events in this book are fictitious.
Any similarity to real persons, living, dead or undead is
coincidental and not intended by the author.

No part of this book may be reproduced in any form or by
any electronic or mechanical means, including information
storage and retrieval systems, without permission in writing
from the publisher, except by a reviewer who may quote
brief passages in a review.

Encyclopocalypse Publications
www.encyclopocalypse.com

The Writer's Cut

Unlike most movie tie-in paperbacks, this book is not a novelization of a screenplay, but simply the screenplay itself.

Let's admit right from the get-go that this is a terrible idea.

For anybody and everybody in the film and TV industries, reading a screenplay is second nature; they've become blind to the formatting—all those CUT TOs and INT. LIVING ROOMs and PAN ACROSSes, all that dialog sitting in the middle of the page instead of safely inside quotation marks, etc.—and can pretty much read a script as easily as they'd read any other long-form narrative; novel, comic book, epic poem, endless twitter-thread, whatever.

But a screenplay is far from a natural form for civilians to read. Their eyes don't recognize the layout of its pages as a story-telling mode, and they're confused by the way it will sometimes break its fourth wall to address them directly. They're right about this latter, of course—while scripts are primarily the telling of a tale, they are also nods, winks, asides, and suggestions to the cast and crew who'll eventually be bringing that tale to life. They're also often peppered with way too many exclamation marks, but that isn't for the sake of the cast and crew. That's for the barely literate MBA grads who become film company executives and who are consistently incapable of recognizing certain things for themselves. Like when something is surprising! Or exciting!! Or terrifying!!! Or big!!!!

So if a screenplay, as a reading experience, is so much trouble for a normal person to get used to, why the hell *isn't* this book a novelization? Believe me, Encyclopocalypse Publications and I would have been delighted if Christian Francis—who did a fantastic job novelizing my *Wishmaster* screenplay for Encyclopocalypse last year—could have taken a shot at this one, too. But we didn't have a choice in the matter. It's actually for a very good reason, though: When Clive Barker created the Hellraiser universe back in the 1980s, he didn't do it by writing and directing the movie *Hellraiser*, he did it by writing the novella *The Hellbound Heart*—which meant that when New World Pictures ponied up the money for the movie rights, Clive retained the *literary* rights. Now while—like any other bite-the-fucking-hand-that-feeds-you screenwriting wretch—I'd have no ethical queasiness about infringing the rights of a film company, infringing the rights of a friend I've known since 1974 is a very different matter. So no novelization. Sorry. (Oh, just to be clear and to save everybody's lawyers a few phone-calls, no film company's rights are being infringed either; Miramax own the copyrighted motion picture *Hellraiser: Bloodline* but—thanks to the separation-of-rights clause in all WGA contracts—writers who earn the single-card credit 'Written By' on a movie retain publication rights to their screenplay.)

Okay. That might explain why this book isn't a *novel*, but it doesn't answer the question as to why we're inflicting it on the world in the first place. Well—and you'll have to pardon me a moment while I get on my high horse—the ridiculous answer is this: public demand.

Not a *big* public, you understand. Quite a tiny one, truth be told. But a deeply invested one. Odds are, in fact, if you've bothered to buy this book, you may be a member of this particular public. You may well be a fan of the first two or three *Hellraiser* movies who found that your relationship with this fourth one was ... well, what shall we say? *Complicated*, maybe? You may, if you were of a kindly and forgiving nature, have found the film somewhat interesting, even occasionally entertaining, but you probably also found it confusing, felt that something just wasn't right about it. You may have noticed the director's name—Alan Smithee—and googled it, and discovered that Alan Smithee doesn't exist, that the name is a pseudonym sometimes applied to movies that have been significantly troubled during production and post-production by crises both financial and creative. You may have, as have many others, expressed a wish that one day perhaps, as a *Hellraiser* fan, you might get to see a Director's Cut of *Bloodline*, the version that was meant to be, the version that its makers originally intended.

I have some bad news.

You'll never see a Director's Cut of *Bloodline*. The footage simply doesn't exist. An assembly could be made that would put the narrative back in somewhat linear form, but it would be missing scores of FX shots and several major sequences. The real director—not Alan Smithee but brilliant special-effects man Kevin Yagher—had his hands tied and his legs cut out from under him by constant studio interference and endless budget cuts. He simply couldn't shoot the movie he'd signed on to direct. And you, sadly, will never get to see it.

But you can read it.

The screenplay published here is the one I wrote in 1995. This is the script that Miramax greenlit, the script that Clive once claimed was the best of the first four Hellraiser screenplays*, and the script that Kevin Yagher fell in love with and was eager to direct. Think of it as the Writer's Cut.

To Kevin—and to all the cast and crew who brought their enormous talents to bear on what sadly turned out to be a cursed production—my love and gratitude. And to you, Hellraiser fan and potential reader, thanks for your interest and affection for all these years. I hope you can find something to enjoy in the screenplay. Think of it as something pulled from the ruins of the movie, as a little glimpse of what might have been.

Peter Atkins,
Los Angeles, October 2021

*I know, I know. He may have been drunk.

HELLRAISER
BLOODLINE
THE ORIGINAL SCREENPLAY

INT. LEMARCHAND'S WORKSHOP - NEARLY MIDNIGHT

RUN TITLES over a series of EXTREME CLOSE-UPS:

- A pair of human hands working delicately on tiny cogs and machinery.
- A human eye grotesquely expanded though a magnifying glass.
- A tiny screwdriver tightening a tiny screw.
- Intricate internal mechanisms of silver, gold and jewels.

INTERCUT with shots of beautiful and intricate automata;

- A Monkey-Musician in blue and gold livery holding a violin.
- A Harlequin holding the hand of a coy Columbine.
- A silver-faced clown perched on a trapeze.

The TITLES end.

WIDEN to reveal the workshop of PHILLIP LEMARCHAND lit by candlelight.

The automata stand on wooden shelves which line the room along with plans and drawings.

At the workbench, Phillip — handsome, 30, obsessed by his craft — is hunched over his work, keeping us from seeing it.

Super-imposed:

THE OUTSKIRTS OF PARIS   1784

There's a strange atmosphere. Perhaps it's the CRAZY SHADOWS thrown by the flickering candles. Perhaps it's the sound of the WIND in the midnight darkness outside. Perhaps it's the amplified HEARTBEAT of Phillip. Something gives an edge to the scene. We're waiting for something to happen.

With a cry of triumph as something clicks into place, Phillip sits back on his chair, his latest creation in his palm.

We recognise the object of black wood and filigreed gold — the LAMENT CONFIGURATION, a hell-summoning Box from HELLRAISER.

The workroom door opens and Phillip's wife GENEVIEVE enters. Mid-20's and beautiful, she is in her nightdress.

>   GENEVIEVE
> Is it done?

>   LEMARCHAND
> Done!

>   GENEVIEVE
>   (yawning)
> Is it wonderful?

>   LEMARCHAND
> Wonderful!

                    GENEVIEVE
                    (smiling)
          Are you brilliant?

                    LEMARCHAND
              (returning the smile)
          The finest toymaker in
          France!

They both laugh affectionately. Beneath their words and their smiles, though, is an undercurrent of ...what? Anxiety? Uncertainty? Perhaps they both sense Phillip is involved in something that he doesn't quite understand.

                    GENEVIEVE
          What does it do?

Proudly, Lemarchand manipulates the Box through various positions until, at a certain point, the mechanisms within seem to take over and it moves itself into the final swastika-like configuration familiar from the previous films...

...and remains sitting on Lemarchand's hand. No chains, no hooks, no blue lights, no screams of pain or pleasure.

The interested smile on Genevieve's face falters.

                    GENEVIEVE
          Oh.
                    (beat)
          It doesn't actually do
          anything, then?

LEMARCHAND
(stung into cold defensiveness)
It all but defies the laws
of physical geometry! It's
my masterpiece! You simply
couldn't understand...

GENEVIEVE
I meant no offense,
Phillip. I'm sure it's
terribly intricate. It's
just... <u>dull</u>. I prefer
your acrobats and lovers.

Laughing disarmingly, she crosses to the shelves and activates some of the older automata. The monkey musician begins to saw at his fiddle. Harlequin kisses Columbine, who hides her blush behind a fan. The Clown swings over and around his trapeze.

Lemarchand, far from placated, is standing and fastening a cloak around himself.

LEMARCHAND
I was working to a
commission. To very
specific requests. The
Duke has what he wanted.

Genevieve registers the cloak as Lemarchand heads for the door.

GENEVIEVE
It's midnight! Where are
you going?

> LEMARCHAND
> The Chateau Du Reve to deliver the box.

> GENEVIEVE
> Now!? Why?

> LEMARCHAND
> Because my work might be appreciated there. And it is the appointed hour.

Opening the door, Box in hand, he sweeps from the room.

Genevieve watches the door close behind him.

> GENEVIEVE
> The appointed hour —
> Midnight! Aristocrats...
> (cont.)

EXT. THE CHATEAU DU REVE - MIDNIGHT

A magnificent mansion stands in its own grounds. Below its lawns is a front gate. A SHADOWY FIGURE hovers at the gate — a beggar or derelict of some kind. The camera moves to show...

Lemarchand at the impressive front door of the Chateau.

> GENEVIEVE
> (cont.) ...Such strange people.

The door is opened by JACQUES, a 19-year-old servant-cum-apprentice to the Chateau's owner — who stands behind him, the powdered and periwigged DUC DE L'ISLE.

De L'Isle's age is hard to determine beneath the layers of white powder that cover his face, but the red and rheumy eyes and spidery limbs suggest he is at least in his late 50s.

From somewhere in the house, a clock tolls midnight.

> DE'L'ISLE
> Lemarchand. As precise as your pieces, as timely as your toys. Enter, enter.

Lemarchand steps over the threshold...

INT. CHATEAU DU REVE, HALLWAY - NIGHT (CONT.)

...into the hall — candle-lit, its outer reaches lost in shadow. There's an impression of decay beneath the finery; a bright light would probably show peeling paint and cobwebs.

De L'Isle's eyes glitter as he looks at the Box in Lemarchand's hand. Beckoning, he leads him across the hall toward a room.

> DE L'ISLE
> Come. Someone is eager to

meet you.

Lemarchand follows, his manner nervous. He is a middle-class artisan in the house of an aristocrat.

Jacques closes the door and looks at Lemarchand and De L'Isle as they walk away. There is a look in his eyes — covetous, ambitious, and secretive.

INT. CHATEAU DU REVE, GAME ROOM - NIGHT (CONT.)

A room lit by many candles, providing a rich atmosphere of contrasting orange light and flickering black shadows.

EIGHT CARDPLAYERS — male, four finely-attired, the other four in military uniform — sit at a large table. A game in progress halts as the players look up as De L'Isle and Lemarchand enter.

>   DE L'ISLE
>   A moment, gentlemen,
>   forgive me. Madame?

A stunningly beautiful woman, emerging from the shadows at the room's end, moves to De L'Isle and Lemarchand.

This is the PRINCESS ANGELIQUE. Dark, mysterious, exquisite.

>   DE L'ISLE
>   Phillip Lemarchand — The

Princess Angelique.

Angelique extends her hand. Lemarchand — visibly struck by her beauty — bends to kiss it. As he straightens, he finds himself the subject of a penetrating stare and a ravishing smile.

>   ANGELIQUE
> Your fame precedes you,
> toymaker.

>   DE L'ISLE
> The Princess is your true
> patron, Lemarchand. The
> Box was her conception,
> your employment her idea.

Lemarchand places the Box in the hands of Angelique.

>   LEMARCHAND
> Though the box is unworthy
> of your beauty, Princess,
> I pray its amusements be
> worthy of your attention.

>   ANGELIQUE
> I thank you, sir. And I
> pray your workmanship
> is as elegant as your
> tongue.

Phillip glows in the warmth of her smile and her words. His face falls, however, as she instantly turns to De L'Isle.

                    ANGELIQUE
              (flatly, unsmiling)
         Pay him.

She turns without another word and moves back into the room, leaving De L'Isle amused at Phillip's obvious disappointment.

                    DE L'ISLE
              Never mistake your
              superior's politeness for
              affection, toymaker. And
              never forget your place.

The sound of a firmly closing door bridges the CUT TO

EXT. THE CHATEAU DU REVE - NIGHT

Lemarchand walks away from the closed front door, his brush with the rich and powerful abruptly over. The path takes him past the lit windows of the game room. He looks in.

INT. CHATEAU DE REVE, GAME ROOM - NIGHT (CONT.)

Jacques fills glasses at a drinks-table. His secretive eyes constantly scour the room — observing, recording, learning.

At the card-table with Angelique, De L'Isle claps his hands for attention and the Players look up at them. We get a clearer look at the Players now and some sense of their personalities:

- CORBUSIER — the natural leader. Rakishly good-looking. Sardonic smile. Cruel eyes. D'Artagnan with a bad attitude.
- DELVAUX — De L'Isle's age but fat, ruddy and libidinous.
- L'ESCARGOT — thin, pinched, and cold. Efficient and amoral. In his next incarnation, an accountant at Auschwitz.
- DE CONDUITE — a dandy. An effeminate heterosexual. Knows a lot about ladies' fashions. Probably collects snuff boxes.
- L'HIVER, PRINTEMPS, L'AUTOMME and L'ETE — young army officers learning the ways of the world from these decadent companions.

                    DE L'ISLE
            Gentlemen: A new game.

Angelique holds the Box up to their collective gaze and hands it to De L'Isle, who passes it on to Corbusier.

A secret look passes between Angelique and De L'Isle — his full of expectation, hers full of promise.

EXT. THE CHATEAU DU REVE - NIGHT (CONT.)

Through the window, Lemarchand sees Corbusier take the Box.

The card-player's mouth moves as if making some comment and we see laughter from his fellows.

It is clear that, though Lemarchand can see the action in the room, he can't hear anything.

INT. CHATEAU DU REVE, GAME ROOM - NIGHT (CONT.)

De L'Isle smiles at whatever witticism Corbusier made.

>DE L'ISLE
>Come, sir. We are all players here. Do we laugh at challenges or accept them?

Corbusier weighs the Box in his hand.

>CORBUSIER
>And what would be the challenge here, De L'Isle? To name this frippery? How about "The Arabian Dice"? — for it is as filigreed as a Moorish temple and as simple as a child's toy.

Amidst the laughter of his fellow players, he rolls it on to the table in contemptuous parody of throwing dice.

Angelique snatches it up. Her icy voice stills the laughter.

>ANGELIQUE
>It already has a name, sir. The Lament Configuration. And as

to being simple... It's
complexity, I wager, is
beyond your skill.

                    CORBUSIER
            (looking her up and down)
            A pretty name, Madame.
            Are the stakes you would
            offer as attractive?

The others giggle at the lascivious
implication in his words.

Angelique silences them with a freezing
glance and then — playing them perfectly —
allows a coy smile to blossom on her face.

She holds the Box up again.

                    ANGELIQUE
            The Box looks solid,
            Gentlemen, but in skilful
            hands may be unlocked and
            maneuvered. Pass it among
            yourselves. For every
            successful stripping of
            its Secrets... I shall
            respond in kind.

To appreciative murmurs from the players,
Angelique raises the Box to her lips and
kisses it.

                    ANGELIQUE
            Now it is complete. Will
            you play, Sir?

She proffers it to Corbusier, who takes

it eagerly and begins to manipulate it, searching for its secrets.

The eyes of the players are fixed on his efforts — so they miss the secret smile that passes between Angelique and De L'Isle. And all of them are blind to the rapt attention of Jacques.

> CORBUSIER
> Ah! There you are!

The Box clicks to a different position. Looking up, he passes the Box carelessly to Delvaux, his expectant eyes on Angelique.

Nodding in acknowledgement, Angelique undoes some catches and removes her dress.

It's 1784, so there are still several layers of undergarments to go. Nevertheless, her action draws smiles from the players and sends Delvaux eagerly to work.

EXT. THE CHATEAU DU REVE - NIGHT (CONT.)

Lemarchand's jaw drops as he sees Angelique disrobe.

(INTERCUT to Lemarchand at various points through the "game")

INT. CHATEAU DU REVE, GAME ROOM - NIGHT (CONT.)

Delvaux works as his fellows watch, quaffing

drinks or taking snuff. L'Escargot is next but it's De Conduite who calls out.

> DE CONDUITE
> Time, sir, time! Pass it on!

L'Escargot reaches for the Box but Delvaux snatches it away.

> DELVAUX
> No! I've nearly... There!!

The Box moves to another setting. All eyes turn lustfully to Angelique as she obligingly removes the first of her petticoats.

> DE L'ISLE
> Play on. Play on.

L'Escargot takes up the Box and begins.

MONTAGE:

- The Box moving from hand to hand, from position to position.
- Angelique removing successive layers of clothing.
- Increasingly-flushed and excited faces.
- A secret excitement growing in De L'Isle's eyes.
- Jacques watching, as excited as his master.
- Lemarchand's face beyond the glass, fascinated and shocked.

Finally, the Box comes back to the hands of Corbusier. He looks at Angelique, now clad only in corset and bloomers.

>CORBUSIER
>It occurs to me, Madame, that should there be more secrets on the table than on the floor, we will need fresh inducement for our endeavours.

>ANGELIQUE
>Oh, there are always more secrets, sir. Always more surprises. Now — will you talk or will you play?

Viciously, Corbusier twists at the Box, seeking one more configuration... and finds it. The Box flies from his hands to the centre of the table — and begins to move *itself*.

>CORBUSIER
>What?

The players all stare in fascination at the moving Box.

>ANGELIQUE
>As I say. Always more secrets. But a wager is a wager...

She begins to loose the catches of her corset.

De L'Isle moves to stand with Jacques.

INTERCUT the Box's movements with the loosening of the corset.

The Box clicks into a penultimate position and BLUE LIGHT glows bright from within it and through the seams at its sides.

Lemarchand is shocked. The Box has secrets its maker didn't suspect. Before he can see more, the drapes suddenly FALL SHUT against the window — as if something knows he's watching.

The players don't notice; breath held, their eyes are on Angelique as she opens her corset to reveal herself...

Her torso transforms — suddenly it is covered in a score of SCREAMING MOUTHS and DEMONIC EYES that stare balefully out into the room. Her FLESH RIPPLES in constant motion as if full of impossible life.

Instantly, the room is full of the AMPLIFIED SOUND OF DEMONIC WHISPERS and bathed in BLUE LIGHT. Angelique's skin takes on a blue tone and her eyes turn completely BLACK. The movements on her chest culminate in a GAPING WOUND that opens there.

Amid CRIES OF HORROR AND FEAR from the cardplayers, the Box clicks into its final position, streaming BLUE LIGHT...

...and the room explodes into hellish and

unnatural life:

- The entire room TREMBLES as if caught in a quake
- Unearthly WINDS explode up from the floor sending the candle flames shooting upwards in powerful RED FIRE, casting NIGHTMARE SHADOWS on the walls.
- Hellish RESTRAINTS shoot from the chairs, twisting around the players' limbs, trapping them in place.
- Overhead, a LARGE WROUGHT-IRON CANDLEABRA hanging from the ceiling moves into a new shape, its eight rococo arms straightening out into viciously SHARP AND POWERFUL LANCES.

The players look up in horror at what has become a killing machine overhead...

...and the CANDLEABRA falls from the ceiling, each of its eight arms heading unerringly for the body of a card-player!

CLOSE on the back and base of a chair as a SPIKE smashes through it, followed by a gush of BLOOD, as we SMASH-CUT TO

EXT THE CHATEAU DU REVE - NIGHT (CONT.)

Lemarchand is some feet back from the curtained window, his face a mask of horror at the TERRIBLE SOUNDS from within the room and the NIGHTMARE SHADOWS playing on the heavy drapes.

Suddenly, the large window SHATTERS OUTWARD

in a massive explosion of light and sound.

Terrified, Lemarchand turns and flees down the garden with the panic-fuelled speed of a man who fears hell is at his heels.

From the gate, he turns into the street and passes the Shadowy Figure we glimpsed earlier. We now see it's A DERELICT with a handcart loaded with junk and curios. The Derelict grabs him.

> DERELICT
> Delicacies, sir? Spices of the orient? Wonders from beyond the sea?

Lemarchand shakes himself free and runs, shouting back.

> LEMARCHAND
> No more wonders! An end to wonders!

The Derelict looks back at the Chateau, blue light pulsing from the windows... And then the light goes out.

INT. CHATEAU DU REVE, GAME ROOM - NIGHT (CONT.)

CLOSE on the Box as it clicks back into its normal position. WIDEN to reveal the room. The Players' chairs are vacant, one or two fallen over as the only testimony to what took place. Jacques is looking at De L'Isle, his face vilely excited.

> DE L'ISLE
> Are you not apprenticed
> to a great magician,
> Jacques?

> JACQUES
> There is indeed great
> magic, sir.

But Jacques is looking at Angelique as he says it.

De L'Isle picks up a chair and rights it. He smiles at Angelique, also back to normal and holding the Box.

> DE L'ISLE
> A fine game, Princess.

> ANGELIQUE
> The first of many, Sir.
> I found a rare talent in
> Lemarchand.

De L'Isle's face becomes cold and imperious.

> DE L'ISLE
> Go to my room, Madam, and
> wait for me.

Oddly, Angelique nods, turns and leaves.

> DE L'ISLE
> (to Jacques)
> He who summons the magic,
> commands the magic. A
> lesson, Jacques.

Jacques nods in understanding.

> CUT TO:

INT. THE SORBONNE ANATOMY CLASS, PARIS – MORNING

CLOSE ON a human arm, as a scalpel slices it and a pair of hands peel the flesh back, revealing the musculature beneath.

WIDEN TO REVEAL a big room, its floor sawdust-covered and blood-soaked, and full of tables on each of which are SHEET-COVERED CORPSES.

At one table, sleeves rolled up and working hard at his dissection, is AUGUSTE DE MARAIS, 30, a professor of science and philosophy. He has no students with him but only his friend Lemarchand. Auguste is smiling broadly, having just heard Lemarchand's story.

(Auguste continues his efficient preparation of the corpse throughout their conversation.)

> AUGUSTE
> A pity Mme. De Beaumont
> is dead these four years.
> You could have sold her
> your story and given
> her another success to
> match her "Beauty and the
> Beast".

LEMARCHAND
It is no story, Auguste!
I saw what I saw, heard
what I heard. The Box
opens the doors of Hell!

AUGUSTE
This is the eighteenth
century, not the dark
ages. The world is ruled
by Reason. We've even got
rid of God. And if there
is no Heaven then it
follows, reasonably, that
there is no Hell.

LEMARCHAND
I was at its very window
last night!

Auguste looks at his friend, hears the conviction in his voice.

AUGUSTE
Very well. Suppose for
the sake of argument that
what you fear happened,
happened. A Box that
<u>opens</u> the doors of Hell
must be able to <u>close</u>
them.

LEMARCHAND
Scant comfort, Auguste.
The Box belongs to people
with little interest in
closing such doors.

> AUGUSTE
> Then the solution lies
> — literally — in your
> hands. You designed a
> machine that you fear can
> bring forth demons.

> LEMARCHAND
> Yes.

> AUGUSTE
> Then design a machine
> that can destroy them.

As Auguste bends down to the difficult (and two-handed) task of pulling the corpse's rib-cage open, Lemarchand stares at his friend, his eyes suddenly excited.

CUT TO:

INT. LEMARCHAND'S WORKROOM - AFTERNOON

The workbench is littered with papers filled with designs and drawings. They reveal a progression from the design of the Lament Configuration towards something else.

Lemarchand works feverishly on a design which completes the process. The six faces of the Box are drawn at the edges of the paper. Lines from points on the faces meet in the centre of the paper to form a shape. From the Box itself has come its own opposite. The new shape, while arising from the Box is antithetical to it; a cat's-cradle of interconnecting and curving lines, rather than a solid and angular mass.

Lemarchand runs his fingers over the shape in the centre of the paper, his eyes burning with the beginning of understanding.

> GENEVIEVE
> (off)
> Phillip? A visitor.

Lemarchand looks up from his desk to the door. Genevieve is there and, beside her, Angelique — at the sight of whom Lemarchand barely manages to conceal his gasp.

> LEMARCHAND
> Princess.

> ANGELIQUE
> Toymaker.

A beat. Angelique looks meaningfully to her side, indicating Genevieve's presence.

> LEMARCHAND
> Thank you, Genevieve.

More eye-language as Genevieve leaves — hers showing anger at being asked to leave, his trying to imply apology.

Angelique watches the door close — and, as Lemarchand gathers up and turns over his drawings to keep them from her eyes, she quietly and secretly turns the key in the door to lock it.

ANGELIQUE
Forgive this unannounced
visit.

LEMARCHAND
An honour. A pleasure.
A... A...

Lemarchand is fumbling. He's afraid. What does this visit mean? Though it's daytime and Angelique is both polite and beautiful, his memory of last night is strong. Angelique moves further in, an amused smile on her lips.

ANGELIQUE
Do I make you nervous?
How delightful.

LEMARCHAND
You took me by surprise.
I was working.

ANGELIQUE
And what work you do,
Phillip. May I call you
Phillip?

He nods.

ANGELIQUE
And you must call me
Angelique.

A beat.

ANGELIQUE
Say it...

She's moved very close to him now. She's almost whispering.

> ANGELIQUE
> ...I want to watch your mouth make the shape of my name.

The light in the room seems to have DIMMED, to have coalesced around them, leaving the rest of the room LOST IN SHADOW. This isn't flirtation. This isn't seduction. This is hypnosis.

Lemarchand is almost dizzy, his fear forgotten.

> LEMARCHAND
> Angelique...

Her eyes fix on his lips as he says it. She's managed to make just the saying of a name an intimate, almost erotic, act.

> ANGELIQUE
> Good. Now we're friends. I much prefer to do business with friends.

> LEMARCHAND
> Business? Were you dissatisfied with the piece I made?

> ANGELIQUE
> I was delighted. Transformed. I want more, Phillip. And so do my

masters.

Phillip gives a quizzical look.

                  ANGELIQUE
Men and women of power. Ready to reward genius. Gold. Fame. The smiles of fair women...

                  LEMARCHAND
I have a wife.

                  ANGELIQUE
Oh. Is _that_ who that was? Well. Whatever. My point is this; I can offer you a world which will appreciate a man of your skills.

                  LEMARCHAND
The Duke is rich, I know, but his influence is not _so_ great.

                  ANGELIQUE
De L'Isle? (laughs) Forget him. An initial contact, that's all. When I say 'Power', I mean real power. And when I say 'Reward', I mean real rewards.

                  LEMARCHAND
Great rewards are usually accompanied by great

                    risks.

                   ANGELIQUE
          Your caution is
          justified. You will hear
          strange stories and see
          strange sights. But <u>you</u>
          are not in danger. You
          are my friend.

She raises her hand to stroke delicately
at his face...

                   ANGELIQUE
          Friends can share things,
          Phillip. Secret things.
          Things even wives needn't
          know.

Their eyes lock. He leans forward, as if
to claim a kiss...

                   GENEVIEVE
                     (off)
             Phillip? Phillip?

CLOSE on the other side of the locked door
— and Genevieve playing with the handle,
concerned.

Inside, the mood changes instantly.
Angelique moves back briskly into the room

— which is suddenly brightly-lit again,
everything back to normal — and heads for
the door.

Lemarchand, head still spinning, calls

after her.

> LEMARCHAND
> Angelique...

She turns at the door, smiling, her hand on the key.

> ANGELIQUE
> Yes?

> LEMARCHAND
> Yes.

> ANGELIQUE
> We shall make great things and see great wonders, you and I.
> (beat)
> Tonight. The Chateau. A masked ball. Come. Meet your patrons. Claim your future.

She unlocks the door and opens it, revealing Genevieve. For a beat, the two women stare at each other. There's a whole conversation in their eyes. And one of it's polite.

Angelique exits, leaving Genevieve staring at her husband.

EXT. LEMARCHAND'S COTTAGE - AFTERNOON (MOMENTS LATER)

As Angelique walks from the front door, she passes another figure heading to it. It is Auguste who, as the ettiquette of the times demand, bows.

Angelique acknowledges the bow but they both stare at each other curiously as if recognising in the other some kind of enmity and, as Auguste walks on to Lemarchand's front door, we CLOSE IN on Angelique's eyes drilling into his back full of a dark and threatening promise.

INT. LEMARCHAND'S WORKROOM AFTERNOON

Lemarchand is gathering up his new sketches, ripping them up and trashing them. Auguste's voice stops him before he reaches the finished design.

> AUGUSTE
> What are you doing?

> LEMARCHAND
> Coming to my senses. You were right. Fairy tales. Tricks of the light.

> AUGUSTE
> Never enter politics, Phillip. Your skill at lying is particularly poor.

Auguste sits. He notices a BLACK FEATHER on the floor, looks briefly puzzled, and then looks at his friend.

AUGUSTE
You had a visitor.

LEMARCHAND
The Princess Angelique.

AUGUSTE
Yes. I rather thought it must have been.
(beat)
Since we spoke, I have heard many whispers in town of the disappearance of eight gamblers.

LEMARCHAND
And this is evidence of what? The Hell in which you don't believe?

AUGUSTE
I'm an atheist, Phillip, not an idiot. Evil is real, whether it wears horns and shakes a trident or flutters its eyelashes and turns the heads of poor craftsmen.

LEMARCHAND
Not poor for long. Tonight I go to the Chateau. To meet patrons and win fame.

AUGUSTE
Good.

Phillip looks surprised.

                    AUGUSTE
          The good man must know
          his enemy. Must look
          it in the face and
          understand it.

Auguste stands up and heads for the door.

                    AUGUSTE
          I shall meet you there
          tonight. And tomorrow we
          shall both meet the day
          with new evidence and new
          understanding.

He leaves. Lemarchand watches him and then looks to his workbench, staring at the cat's-cradle design.

                                        CUT TO:

EXT. WOODS NEAR PARIS LATE AFTERNOON.

Auguste walks through a deserted wood. The sunlight has a strange quality — pregnant with darkness, ready for twilight.

A large BLACK BIRD flies and lands on a high branch. It seems to be staring at Auguste...

As Auguste turns into a clearing, there is a WHOOSH of sound and a FLURRY of movement.

Auguste starts back with a gasp. The

movement resolves into AN ACROBAT tumbling through the air in a cartwheel dive and landing upright, grinning madly, a foot in front of Auguste.

LAUGHTER and APPLAUSE draw Auguste's eyes forward:

Stretched between two trees is a painted-sheet backdrop. Before it, a TROUPE OF CLOWNS, the traditional figures of 18th century Commedia Dell'Arte: HARELQUIN, COLUMBINE, PIERROT, PULCINELLA, and THE SURGEON, along with four ACROBATS. Their costumes are even more exaggerated and bizarre than normal, and they all have strange half-smiles, as if they possess a secret knowledge. Or are close to the borders of sanity.

The Surgeon — a comically grotesque short man with tiny glittering eyes and an absurdly full beard — walks forward.

>   SURGEON
> As the day is long, sir,
> an excellent surprise.
> And most welcome.
>   (he bows to Auguste)
> You have stumbled, sir,
> upon Europe's finest
> comedians.

>   AUGUSTE
> Comedians? Here?

On the branch, the Black Bird observes the action.

SURGEON
So it appears, sir,
yes. And should we be
elsewhere?

AUGUSTE
I have no idea. I,
however, should be. I
have a class to teach.

SURGEON
We too have an
appointment, sir. But
regrettably have eaten
our map.
        (he belches)
Perhaps you could help.
Are you a local man, sir?

The day is growing darker. And there's something increasingly unsettling about the silent unwavering smiles of the Clowns.

AUGUSTE
   (nods)
I am Auguste de Marais,
Philosopher.

SURGEON
Philosophy! A fine trade,
and never to be confused
with the training of
frogs, which is — I speak
from experience — a much
overrated profession.

AUGUSTE
With respect, I have

> no time to discuss the
> relative virtues of men's
> careers. To where do you
> wish to be directed?
>
>   SURGEON
> To the Chateau Du Reve,
> sir. We are to perform at
> a great masked ball.
>
>   AUGUSTE
> You are but a mile away.
> Clear the wood and you
> shall see it.
>
>   SURGEON
>   (speaking with gratitude)
> Your kindness must be
> rewarded, sir. Players!
> Prepare!

The Clowns draw two TRUMPETS and a BASS DRUM from a sack.

>   AUGUSTE
> I thank you. But you must
> excuse me.
>
>   SURGEON
> And leave you unsatisfied,
> sir? An unsatisfied
> audience is the saddest
> thing in the world, save
> a one-legged fish in a
> barrel of pork.
>
>   AUGUSTE
> I assure you. There is no

need.

                    SURGEON
          But I insist.

Suddenly, from his coat, the Surgeon produces two gleaming BUTCHER'S KNIVES which he holds upright, one in each hand.

The Acrobat near Auguste does a backflip and ends up behind the startled Philosopher, blocking his path.

                    SURGEON
          A brief diversion in
          your busy day, sir. An
          entertainment entitled
          YOUR LAST SIGHT ON EARTH
          and guaranteed to please.
                    (to troupe)
          Music!

Pierrot and Pulcinella blow trumpets. An Acrobat pounds the drum. The music is piercing and discordant.

Another Acrobat somersaults swiftly to Auguste and, held tight by an Acrobat on each side, he is carried to the backdrop...

...where Harlequin and Columbine are in a pantomime argument. Harlequin, with angry looks and pointing fingers, is accusing. Columbine, with fervent eyes and imploring hands, is denying.

The acrobats bring Auguste on 'stage'. Columbine GASPS. Harlequin gestures at him accusingly.

Columbine, blushing prettily, can deny no longer. Staring at Auguste, her hands flutter over her heart and an exaggeratedly dreamy look fills her face. Yes, this is her secret lover.

> AUGUSTE
> Enough! Let me go!!

Shocked, Columbine and Harlequin put their fingers to their lips. One of the acrobats stuffs a small red ball in Auguste's mouth to keep him quiet.

The Black Bird keeps watching as the show continues.

Harlequin confers silently with the Surgeon, now on stage. The Surgeon, sympathetic, offers one of his knives. Harlequin looks at the knife, at Auguste, shakes his head.

The Surgeon produces a duelling pistol from his pocket. Harlequin shakes his head.

The Surgeon tries again and produces a lobster and some cheese. Harlequin gives him a look.

The Surgeon has a bright idea. He points to the sheet backdrop. Harlequin nods excitedly and gestures to the two acrobats holding Auguste.

The Acrobats lift Auguste up into the air, his stifled CRIES OF DENIAL coming from behind the ball-gag.

A drum-roll and a flourish of atonal trumpets...

Harlequin and the Surgeon each grasp a side of the sheet...

The Acrobats swing Auguste through the air... once... twice...

The backdrop sheet is whipped away...

...revealing a HUGE MAW OF HELL. Denying physical reality, it stretches back into a dark infinity like an impossible tunnel opened between dimensions. Circular, ribbed, and pulsing, it resembles a GIANT OESOPHAGOUS. The mouth/entrance is a blur of terrifying activity — hundreds of long sharp objects rotate wildly like the blades of some VAST ORGANIC THRESHING MACHINE.

The Black Bird beats its wings and flies from the branch.

Auguste is hurled directly at the maw, muffled SCREAMS OF HORROR coming from his mouth, limbs twitching in protest.

The Troupe LAUGH and APPLAUD as we SMASH-CUT TO BLACK

EXT. LEMARCHAND'S COTTAGE - NIGHT

The BLACKNESS resolves into a NIGHT SKY above the cottage.

INT. LEMARCHAND'S BEDROOM NIGHT

Lemarchand, eyes open, is lying with his arm around Genevieve, who is asleep. A beat, and he takes his arm away, slips quietly from the bed, and begins dressing in the semi-darkness.

He hasn't got far before Genevieve sits up in bed.

>   LEMARCHAND
> I didn't want to wake
> you. I--
>
>   GENEVIEVE
>   (interrupting)
> You're as automatic as
> one of your toys! She
> turns your key, and you
> perform!
>
>   LEMARCHAND
> You're being ridiculous.
> You refuse to see what
> this could mean for us.
>
>   GENEVIEVE
> I know what she means for
> us!
>
>   LEMARCHAND
> You'd have me turn my
> back on fortune because

                    of some petty female
                    jealousy!

                              GENEVIEVE
                    It isn't that! It isn't
                    just that. It's that
                    place. Those people.

                              LEMARCHAND
                    "Those people" are going
                    to give me--

                              GENEVIEVE
                        (interrupting)
                    A son?! Because that's
                    what I'm going to give
                    you, Phillip! A son.

A beat. He stares at her, anger replaced by incredulous happiness. He clambers on the bed to fling his arms round his wife, who is somewhere between laughter and tears at the strength of his reaction.

                              LEMARCHAND
                    This is wonderful. Are
                    you sure?

She nods happily. He kisses her forehead.

                              LEMARCHAND
                    All the more reason I
                    must go.

He stands to leave.

                              GENEVIEVE
                    No! You belong here! With

>   me. With us.
>
>   LEMARCHAND
>   We belong together. But
>   not here. My son will be
>   born in a palace! Built
>   by the fortune I go to
>   claim tonight.

He flings the bedroom door open and is gone. Genevieve stares at the closed door, distraught.

>   GENEVIEVE
>   No. No!

                                        CUT TO:

EXT. THE CHATEAU DE REVE - NIGHT

The Chateau sits atop its hilled gardens, framed by a night sky where heavy grey clouds gather oppressively, presaging thunder.

In the distance, still peddling his wares, the Derelict.

INT. CHATEAU DU REVE, BALLROOM - NIGHT

Lemarchand enters the Ballroom, a space of smoke and laughter and the chink of wine glasses. MUSICIANS play. Jacques serves drinks. There are sixteen guests, eight men, eight women. All are elaborately MASKED, but the eight men seem familiar —

they are the GAMBLERS.

Lemarchand, startled by the grotesque masks and drunken laughter, moves through the ballroom, looking for Angelique.

He sees movement through a connecting door and walks through...

INT. CHATEAU DU REVE, ANTE-ROOM - NIGHT (CONT.)

...into a dimly lit room with very little furniture. On a small table is the Box, a few candles burning around it.

A circular rug sits in the centre of the floor.

Angelique's there, holding a thin wand connected to a bird-mask in front of her face. Her mask and costume are black and feathered, reminding us of the bird that watched Auguste die.

Lemarchand bows courteously. She places her hand on his arm and moves in very close to him.

>   ANGELIQUE
> I knew you'd come. You're
> a brave man, Phillip.
>
>   LEMARCHAND
> Not so brave. It would be
> a foolish man who ignored
> the promise of success.

ANGELIQUE
Then the world is full of fools.

LEMARCHAND
Or empty of promise.

ANGELIQUE
No. The promise is everywhere. Success is limited only by desire. The wise man sees that. The brave man acts on it.

LEMARCHAND
Then so far I may have been wise. But not yet brave.

Angelique tilts her beautiful head and pulls aside the mask.

ANGELIQUE
Be brave...

She's irresistible. Their mouths meet in a deep slow kiss...

Suddenly, THREE GUESTS in a drunken gavotte spill in from the ballroom, nearly colliding into them. One of them spies Angelique's face. We recognise the voice behind the mask.

CORBUSIER
Ah! Our Lady of the Labyrinth!

Swept into formation, she's spun out of the room. Lemarchand, dizzy from the kiss, is startled by a VOICE from the shadows.

> DE L'ISLE
> What did she taste of, toymaker?

De L'Isle walks forward, turning up the wick on an oil-lamp he carries to show himself more clearly. Unlike his guests, he is unmasked — though his face is twisted in suppressed rage.

> LEMARCHAND
> My apologies, you excellency. I thought we were alone.

> DE L'ISLE
> Tasted sweet, didn't she? Vanilla. To hide the stench of death. Come here.

Waving the oil-lamp, he beckons Lemarchand to the middle of the room. He angles the light down toward the floor...

...and yanks away the circular rug, revealing a large painted pattern on the wooden slates — a five-pointed star within a circle. A Pentagram.

> DE L'ISLE
> That's what your Box is designed to replace. That and a few words of

                    Old Latin. Such outmoded
                    medieval methods.

                              LEMARCHAND
                    Methods of what?

                              DE L'ISLE
                                (sneers)
                    You really don't know
                    what you've gotten
                    yourself into, do you?
                                (a beat)
                    Methods of summoning
                    creatures from Hell.

He lifts the light to their faces — his amused, Lemarchand's appalled.

                                        CUT TO:

INT. LEMARCHAND'S WORKROOM - NIGHT

The camera roams, moving to the workbench — where we see again the cat's-cradle design — and round to reveal Genevieve. As she scans the room, looking at Phillip's designs and sketches, she is putting on a cloak. Her face is set in a determined mask. She's going to fetch her husband back.

                                        CUT TO:

INT. CHATEAU DU REVE, ANTE-ROOM NIGHT

The lamp is on the floor. De L'Isle has

picked up the Box and is bouncing it in his hand as he walks towards Lemarchand, who backs away, both describing a circle around the Pentagram.

> DE L'ISLE
> I introduced her to your skill. Little did I know that your science was to replace my magic.

> LEMARCHAND
> You misunderstand. The Princess has offered me more work, that's all.

> DE L'ISLE
> There'd be no end of work, toymaker, no end of work. They're full of ideas. Always have been. But they needed a human genius to make their ideas manifest. How they must have longed for History to deliver them one such as you.

Face creased with anger, he hurls the Box at Lemarchand's face. Lemarchand blocks it, catches it, and looks up to see that De L'Isle has drawn a long and lethal dagger from his belt.

> DE L'ISLE
> But I'm not ready to retire.
> (gestures to the Pentagram)

> That's where I summoned
> her. That's where I'll
> send her back... Once
> I've killed you!

He lunges viciously. Lemarchand throws himself back, avoiding the knife but losing his footing and falling to the floor.

De L'Isle moves in, towering menacingly above Lemarchand...

...and is suddenly seized from behind by Angelique, whose face is contorted in cold fury. She grasps the knife hand and SNAPS HIS WRIST easily!

De L'Isle cries out in pain and cringes visibly, backing away as Angelique advances on him.

> ANGELIQUE
> A true magician never
> forgets the rules. A
> summoned demon is yours to
> command forever — unless
> you stand in hell's way.
> Hell needs this man. And
> I no longer need you...

She grasps De L'Isle by the throat, hoists him impossibly high with one hand, and effortlessly flings him more than thirty feet to SMASH through a glass window at the far end of the room.

Almost as an afterthought, she clicks her fingers...

...and magically, the huge curtains gathered to each side of the window unfurl and close over the shattered glass.

Lemarchand rises to his feet as she moves toward him.

> ANGELIQUE
> Dancing with another. Do you toy with my jealousy, Phillip?

She laughs. Lemarchand doesn't. He backs away from her... and into the painted pattern of the Pentagram.

Angelique freezes on the edge of the pattern. It's clear she can't — or won't — enter. She smiles beguilingly and holds her arms out to Lemarchand.

> ANGELIQUE
> I confess, sir, your kiss has confirmed the promise of your eyes. I burn for you, my love. Come to me.

> LEMARCHAND
> (flat and final)
> I think not, Madame.

Instantly, the siren-side of Angelique disappears. She drops her arms and her smile and is all business.

> ANGELIQUE
> Well. To commerce. You have a talent. I have

                    a fortune. State your
                    terms.

                         LEMARCHAND
                    I think not, Madame.

Angelique's face clouds with cold fury.

                         ANGELIQUE
                    Think again, Sir.

Lemarchand's silence is eloquent.

                         ANGELIQUE
                    Neither pleasure nor
                    fortune persuades
                    you? Then we must try
                    something else.

She clicks her fingers as she did before.

Instantly, the closed curtains fly open with a flourish like the curtains of a theatre...

...and they don't give on to a shattered window but to an IMPOSSIBLY LONG CORRIDOR disappearing into a dark distance. And from it into the room comes the Troupe of Clowns. Two Acrobats blow discordant trumpets and two more beat bass drums.

Lemarchand stares in shock and fear as the Clowns produce their knives and smile their maniac smiles.

Suddenly, one of the Acrobats frees his Bass Drum and rolls it swiftly at Lemarchand.

It hits his feet, falls to its side...

...and reveals that it's made of HUMAN SKIN — and, in the middle, still hideously recognisable, are the STRETCHED AND TORTURED FEATURES OF AUGUSTE.

Lemarchand staggers back — and out of the Pentagram.

Angelique steps in front of him, her face creased in a sadistic grin, as the Clowns spread out into the room behind her.

Lemarchand's eyes dart everywhere — judging distances.

> ANGELIQUE
> And what do you think
> now, sir?

> LEMARCHAND
> I thank God my poor dead
> friend guided my hand to
> better work this morning!

> ANGELIQUE
> What do you mean?

As he answers, Angelique's face clouds in fury and suspicion.

> LEMARCHAND
> I mean that everything
> made may be unmade. That
> everything open may be
> closed.

And suddenly he makes his break, running madly for the door to the Ballroom before any of the Clowns can reach him.

But, to the sound of Angelique's demonic LAUGHTER, the door opens from the far side and the eight masked gamblers rush in.

Lemarchand stops and stares at the gamblers...

...as they rip the masks from their faces, revealing the GROTESQUE PALLOR and HIDEOUS SCARS of their dead faces.

>   ANGELIQUE
>   As promised, gentlemen. A
>   new game!

The faces of the ZOMBIE GAMBLERS break into cruel and hungry grins as they advance toward Lemarchand.

EXT. THE CHATEAU DU REVE - NIGHT

Genevieve, moving through the gardens in the moonlit darkness, is pressing her way through a thicket.

We are CLOSE on her face...

on her hands...

on her foot...

...as a HAND suddenly shoots from the undergrowth and grabs her ankle.

Genevieve SCREAMS and jerks herself free, running furiously up the path towards the front door.

Behind her, dragging himself from the undergrowth, we see De L'Isle, badly cut and bruised.

At the front door, Genevieve pounds on it and gets no response. Trying the handle, she finds it's unlocked and lets herself in.

INT. CHATEAU DU REVE, HALLWAY - NIGHT (CONT.)

Genevieve pauses in the unlit hallway, unsure of where to go. She sees a faint light coming from a room in the distance.

INT. CHATEAU DU REVE, ANTE-ROOM - NIGHT

Genevieve creeps into the room, still lit by the oil-lamp and apparently empty except for a bundle of rags on the floor... which suddenly murmurs her name.

>   TORTURED VOICE
>   Genevieve...

With a cry, Genevieve moves nearer to the shape on the floor. It is Lemarchand, horribly wounded and very close to death.

>   GENEVIEVE
>   No! No! Phillip!

Genevieve falls to her knees, cradling her poor husband's head in her arms. Panic crosses what's left of Lemarchand's face.

He presses the Box into her hands.

>   LEMARCHAND
>   Genevieve! Get out!
>   Save yourself! Save the
>   child...

>   ANGELIQUE
>   (off)
>   Child?

Suddenly, Angelique and the Gamblers are in the room. Delvaux and Corbusier grab Genevieve and drag her to her feet.

Despair crosses Lemarchand's face and he finally dies.

>   GENEVIEVE
>   Phillip!

Genevieve sobs. Angelique moves to her, sadistic triumph on her face.

>   GENEVIEVE
>   What kind of monster are
>   you?!

>   ANGELIQUE
>   The careful kind. Phillip
>   Lemarchand can have no
>   child. His bloodline
>   must die with him lest
>   his genius be reborn and

turned against us.

> GENEVIEVE
> No! You can't!

> ANGELIQUE
> Believe me, I can.

Fingers bent into claws, she moves toward Genevieve...

...as De L'Isle hurtles into frame, seizing Angelique.

With the advantage of surprise and momentum, he propels both himself and the Princess into the Pentagram where, before any of the Gamblers can react, he shouts out a Latin revocation.

> DE L'ISLE
> Exeunt Omnia Malefica!

All the Gamblers devolve instantly into HUMAN-SHAPED TOWERS OF WORMS, each a mass of pink and brown writhing shapes which drop to the floor, where their wrigglings are overtaken by a collective transformation into LUMPS OF PRIMAL OOZE...

...which, in turn, become PILES OF DRY DUST which, seized by supernatural wind, are swept away into nothingness.

Simultaneously, Angelique SCREAMS... and EXPANDS, her body MORPHING impossibly into a huge mass of DEMONIC EYES and SCREAMING DEMONIC MOUTHS — an even more nightmarish version of the revelation she gave the gamblers the previous night.

There is a BLINDING FLASH OF LIGHT...

And suddenly, Genevieve is completely alone in the room.

Still holding the Lament Configuration, she turns and flees.

EXT. CHATEAU DE REVE - NIGHT

As Genevieve turns into the street, she is startled by the Derelict. He goes into his usual rap.

> DERELICT
> Wonders, Madam? Spices of
> the orient? Perfumes from
> far Cathay?

Genevieve looks at him. She looks at the Box in her hand. She looks at the Chateau and its memories of evil. She hands the Box to the startled and delighted Derelict and leaves.

INT. CHATEAU DU REVE, ANTE-ROOM - NIGHT

SERIES OF CLOSE-UPS: A hand lights many candles. The Pentagram is sprinkled with salt. An ancient-looking book is opened to a page of Latin manuscript.

Latin words are intoned monosyllabically.

There is a burst of light...

...and Angelique is back within the Pentagram. She looks startled, glancing round the room, confused.

Jacques, the apprentice, is standing outside the pentagram. It is he who has staged the ritual.

> JACQUES
> Welcome, Princess.

> ANGELIQUE
> You? You summoned me?

> JACQUES
> And he who summons the
> magic, commands the
> magic. You belong to me.
> Forever.

Angelique's face falls. Have her great ambitions come to this?

> JACQUES
> And I will never make
> De L'Isle's mistake,
> Princess. Count on that.

He begins to laugh as he draws her from the Pentagram and strokes her face in proprietary lust.

CUT TO:

EXT. THE ATLANTIC OCEAN - DAY

A large wood-built sailing ship heads west.

Super-imposed:

> *THE CLIPPER "LIBERTE",*
> *EN ROUTE TO NEW YORK.*

INT. "LIBERTE", SMALL CABIN - DAY

The very pregnant Genevieve sit sin her tiny cabin. She is reading intently in a small leather-bound volume. On the cover are the words *Le Journal de Phillip Lemarchand*. We see the concentration on her face and the scrawled and detailed handwriting that fills the volume's pages.

The room contains suitcases, trunks, one of Lemarchand's creations (perhaps the monkey-musician... and a large document stretched out on the cabin's tiny table.

It's the cat's-cradle design. We TRACK IN to an EXTREME CLOSE UP, closer and closer until the BLACKNESS of a single ink line FILLS THE SCREEN...

INT. BLACKNESS/DREAM-SPACE

...and suddenly the BLACKNESS is replaced by a RAPID MONTAGE OF IMAGES.

At first, the images are familiar — it's

like a fast-forward through the story we've just seen: The Box, Nightmare Clowns, Zombie Gamblers, Angelique's face, etc. Then others are added to the mix —

- a half-glimpsed CENOBITE BEAST, terrifying but shadowed.
- a GRANDMOTHER (vaguely familiar — like Genevieve at 75) looking down as if speaking to a child's POV.

                    GRANDMOTHER
            You're the one, Johnny.
            You're the one they've
            been waiting for...

- Elevator doors clanging together and a VOID behind them.

The images flick back and forth, faster and faster, achieving a nightmare crescendo, until suddenly the BLACKNESS returns, a MALE VOICE SCREAMS, and we...

INT. MERCHANT'S APARTMENT, BEDROOM - NIGHT

...TRACK OUT of the SCREAMING MOUTH of JOHN MERCHANT.

It's 4 a.m. and John blinks his nightmare away as his wife, BOBBI, clicks on a bedside light to reveal a modern-day apartment bedroom.

                    BOBBI
            Honey? You okay? Another

dream?

> JOHN
> Yeah. Another dream. Or the same one.

Bobbi's an attractive mid-20's woman. John's... very familiar looking. In fact, apart from the 20th century haircut, he's a dead ringer for Phillip Lemarchand.

Suddenly, the sound of more screams. Not John this time.

> JOHN
> Oh, shit. I woke Jack. Again.

Bobbi's already out of bed. John gets up and follows her through to...

INT. MERCHANT'S APARTMENT, JACK'S ROOM (CONT.)

...the bedroom of JACK, their 7-year-old, who, woken and disturbed by his father's screams, is sitting on his bed.

Bobbi and John rush over to him, Bobbi comforting him with an embrace while John looks apologetically distressed.

> BOBBI
> There, there, sweetie. It's okay.

                    JOHN
          I'm sorry, partner. Don't
          be scared. Just Daddy
          having bad dreams again.

                    BOBBI
          And dreams can't hurt
          you, darling.

                    JOHN
          They can't hurt anybody.

Bobbi has got Jack back beneath the covers.
He's already sleepy again but he looks up
at his father.

                    JACK
          Not even you, daddy?

                    JOHN
          No. No, not even me.

Jack's eyes close as Bobbi strokes his
brow. He seems comforted by his father's
assurance but, as Bobbi and John find each
other's worried eyes, we see that they are
less sure than their words imply.

                                   CUT TO:

EXT. CHATEAU DU REVE - DAY

The Chateau looks identical to when we
last saw it — except that it now stands in
20th Century surroundings.

                               DISSOLVE TO:

INT. CHATEAU DU REVE, ANTE-ROOM - DAY

The anteroom is now decorated as a modern-day living room. Jacques and Angelique are there. Angelique, unchanged by the centuries, is as beautiful as ever.

Jacques, too, looks the same but there is a terrible corrupt decadence in his eyes. He is sitting at a table messily finishing a greasy meal. Angelique watches in disgust.

>   ANGELIQUE
>   Do you know what I loathe
>   most about you?

>   JACQUES
>   (between mouthfuls)
>   "Do you know what I
>   loathe most about you,
>   <u>master</u>?"

>   ANGELIQUE
>   Master. It's your lack of
>   ambition. Have you sought
>   power? Influence? Fame?
>   No. You--

Jacques has a last swallow, belches, and interrupts.

>   JACQUES
>   Shut up.

Angelique falls silent.

>   JACQUES

            Do the dishes.

Angelique waves a hand. The grease-stained plates and cups are suddenly sparkling-clean and neatly stacked on the table.

                    JACQUES
        (putting a cigarette in his mouth)
            Light me.

Another wave. The cigarette tip glows magically into life. Jacques takes a deep satisfying drag and looks at her.

                    JACQUES
            Good. Now get down on
            your hands and knees and
            ask me to hurt you. And
            ask nicely.

Angelique's enraged eyes don't stop her body from doing as it's told. Jacques smiles cruelly as he crosses toward her.

                                    CUT TO:

INT. MERCHANT'S APARTMENT - DAY

Bobbi and John sit at the breakfast table. Bobbi throws a glance to check Jack is sufficiently engrossed in his toys at the far end of the room and then turns to John.

                    BOBBI
            You look terrible.

JOHN
(smiling)
Love you, too.

BOBBI
I'm worried. You should see someone.

JOHN
You know I've had them all my life.

BOBBI
As often? As bad?

John shakes his head.

BOBBI
It's your goddam grandmother.

JOHN
She was a wonderful woman.

BOBBI
She was a weird woman. All those stories. How important your family is. How important you are. She put stuff in your mind, John.

JOHN
Not all of it. There's stuff there that feels like... memories. Impossible memories. And

>   they don't just haunt my
>   dreams. They haunt my
>   work. Everything I've
>   done...

He trails off, as if it's impossible to explain.

>   BOBBI
>   I don't want you haunted.
>   I don't want you hurt.
>
>   JOHN
>   It's not that. It's
>   stress. This Award
>   Banquet tonight. I hate
>   shit like that.
>
>   BOBBI
>   (smiling proudly)
>   Then you shouldn't be so
>   good.
>
>   JOHN
>   I'm not. I'm not even
>   sure I deserve the award.
>
>   BOBBI
>   Right. That's why of all
>   the buildings in the
>   country, yours was voted
>   the best.

Bobbi picks up a magazine from the table and throws it to him.

>   JOHN
>   Hey, I didn't say I

>   wasn't better than
>   everyone else. I just
>   said I could be better. I
>   could've made it perfect.

CLOSE on John as he picks up the magazine and we CUT TO...

INT. CHATAEU DU REVE, ANTE-ROOM - DAY

...CLOSE on a magazine cover with a photo of John in the lobby of a building. We saw the lobby at the end of Hellraiser III. The massive murals that cover the walls are all based on the Lament Configuration. Cover-copy over the photo reads *La Nouvelle Décor Americain: John Merchant et su Chef de l'Oeuvre*.

PULL BACK to reveal Angelique holding the magazine. She is staring, stunned, at John and the lobby. Her fingers trace over the cover.

>   ANGELIQUE
>   (to herself)
>   At last. A purpose. A
>   reason...

Her reverie is interrupted by the sound of Jacques' entrance. She lays the magazine down and looks across at him.

>   ANGELIQUE
>   I'm restless. And you're
>   bored. Why don't we take
>   a trip?

JACQUES
We took a trip. India.

ANGELIQUE
That was in 1949! I think
we should see America.

JACQUES
Screw America. All they
want to talk about is how
they won the war for us.

ANGELIQUE
Then I would like your
permission to go by
myself.

JACQUES
No.

ANGELIQUE
Short and to the point.
Is that your final word?

JACQUES
Yes.

ANGELIQUE
Good.

There's something in how she said that
that gets Jacques' attention. He looks at
her searchingly.

ANGELIQUE
You remember De L'Isles's
mistake? The one you said
you'd never make?

A smile is blooming on Angelique's face. Jacques' jaw drops. His eyes flick nervously from side to side.

> ANGELIQUE
> You seem tense. In need of relaxation. Why not ask me to do something vile and degrading? That usually works.

Jacques' fear grows.

> JACQUES
> Angelique... I... Please...

> ANGELIQUE
> You're blubbering like a little boy, <u>Master</u>.
> (a beat)
> Act your age.

And he does. With a snap of her fingers, Jacques BEGINS TO AGE — a second for every year he has lived.

Within moments, he is a wrinkled, toothless, rheumy-eyed old man.

> JACQUES
> No! No, please! It hurts!!

> ANGELIQUE
> A summoned demon is yours to command forever. Unless you stand in Hell's way.

>   Hell's game is afoot in
>   America. I'd send you a
>   post-card, but...

The process continues. Jacques is impossibly ancient — 150 years old, 180, 200...

>   JACQUES
>   Aaargh!!!!

>   ANGELIQUE
>   ...you won't be around to
>   read it.

For a second, the 230-year-old Jacques stands staring in horror at Angelique, and then finally collapses, crumbling to the floor like a long-dead corpse.

>   CUT TO:

EXT. THE BUILDING - NIGHT

An office-building framed against the sky. A line of Limos deposits smartly dressed people beside the forecourt.

From OFF, the sound of APPLAUSE...

>   TIME-DISSOLVE:

INT. THE BUILDING, LOBBY - NIGHT

The lobby — dominated by its magnificent Box-like murals — is set up for the awards banquet. Many dining tables fill the centre of the space before a raiser platform on which stands a lectern with a microphone and a computer console.

The invited guests are finishing coffee and applauding as John approaches the lectern.

John looks around at the sea of faces. He's nervous. Not a public man. He clears his throat and leans to the mike.

> JOHN
> Erm... well... thanks.

Nervous laugh from John. Supportive laughs from the audience.

> JOHN
> I've always thought the applause of your peers is the best kind of applause so I'm particularly touched by your response and by the award. I think that... Well, when I... What I'm trying to say... Ah, if I'd been any good with words I would've written books. I make things. And you're sitting in the middle of something I made. So I'll let it do my talking, if that's okay.

John turns to the console on the lectern and keys something in.

Members of the audience look puzzled. They glance at each other. They glance at John. They glance at the walls of the lobby. A sense of embarassment is growing...

...replaced by a sense of awe: Cued by a very quiet engine-like noise, the audience turns to look at the back wall. Framed high in the centre of an otherwise blank wall is a large square-shaped Box-like design — which begins to move! By some clever trick of engineering, the design within changes constantly. It's almost like they're looking at an animated film image, except the design is physically moving.

Gasps and cries of delight burst from the audience and a huge wave of appreciative applause fills the lobby.

> JOHN
> See, the building was
> ready for occupancy
> before this was finished.

John's voice fills the hall, but people aren't listening to him. They're lost in the splendour of his creation.

> JOHN
> I felt kind of fraudulent
> taking this award
> because... because...

John is blinking, losing his train of thought. Something's the matter. We see the lobby from his POV —

— It's _too_ dazzling, _too_ impressive. Lights, bouncing off the moving panel, glitter and reflect off the metallic surfaces of the other murals. They refract and reflect in an almost blinding coruscation of light. The sounds in the room take on an ARTIFICIAL ECHO, laughter and applause reverberating like in a bad acid-trip.

John stumbles for his words, bemused and bedazzled.

> JOHN
> See, it's still not finished... not Perfect... there was... I...

John, blinking and twitching, glances round the room through his distorted perspective. He's trying to find something to anchor on, something to stop the confusion of sight and sound.

ANGLE ON Bobbi and Jack in the audience. Bobbi's looking concerned at the podium. It's clear John can't see her.

> BOBBI
> (to Jack)
> C'mon, honey.

She helps Jack to his feet and begins to lead him away.

> JACK
> Aren't we waiting for daddy?

                    BOBBI
          We're getting the car,
          sweetheart. Daddy wants
          to leave.

ANGLE ON John, still confused and disoriented. He puts a hand to his forehead to shield his eyes. What's happening to him?

Suddenly, his eyes lock on a face in the crowd — a face that, unlike every other in the room, is staring directly at him.

It's Angelique.

John stares at this beguiling, smiling woman in confusion. Who is she? Where does he know her from?

Angelique's mysterious knowing stare doesn't falter. Finally, John looks away to mumble into the mike.

                    JOHN
          Erm... So, thanks.
          Thanks...

He steps off the platform, head spinning, and walks rapidly away toward the exit door.

EXT. THE BUILDING - NIGHT

John staggers out onto the deserted forecourt and moves to the edge of the sidewalk, turning his head up to the night to gulp in some air and get himself steady.

Angelique exits through the revolving doors. She's many yards behind John and unseen by him. She spots John and, face set in threatening determination, heads rapidly towards him...

Suddenly, a uniformed VALET-PARKER steps right in her path.

> VALET
> Ma'am. Do you have your-?

Angelique's concentration is broken for a second. She stares angrily at the Valet and pushes him aside.

> VALET
> Hey!

Angelique looks back to where John was...

...only to see him disappearing into the back of a Limo.

Snarling in frustration, Angelique watches the Limo pull away.

TIME-DISSOLVE:

INT. THE BUILDING, LOBBY - NIGHT

It's later. The lobby is all but deserted. UNIFORMED HELP stack tables and chairs. Three or four STRAGGLING GUESTS hover near the door ready to leave.

One guest, SHARPE, a 40-year-old man, glances round the lobby. A figure in the shadows at the far end catches his eye. It's Angelique. She fixes Sharpe's gaze with a look at once challenging and inviting.

Sharpe looks to right and left. Nobody is paying any attention to either him or this beautiful stranger. With a small maybe-I-just-got-lucky smile, he makes his way across the lobby.

                              CROSS-FADE TO:

INT. SERVICE STAIRWELL - NIGHT

Angelique leads Sharpe down a dimly lit stairwell towards the basements of the building.

> SHARPE
> At least tell me your name.

> ANGELIQUE
> Do we really need to know each other's names?

> SHARPE
> A mystery woman, eh?

> ANGELIQUE
> Aren't you excited by mystery?

                    SHARPE
            Oh yeah. You bet.

They've reached a door at the bottom of the
stairwell. Sharpe reaches for Angelique.
She pulls away, gesturing at the door.

                    ANGELIQUE
            In here.

                    SHARPE
              (opening the door)
            You seem pretty familiar
            with this place.

They walk through the door...

INT. THE BUILDING, BASEMENT - (CONT.)

...into the basement of the building.

                    ANGELIQUE
            No. I'm just following my
            instincts.

                    SHARPE
            Me too.

Angelique doesn't mean quite what he
thinks; she's glancing round like a hound
on the scent. Unerringly, she heads for a
large bare concrete pillar at the corner
of the basement. She lays her hand on it,
barely concealed excitement on her face.

                    ANGELIQUE
            Do you like games?

                    SHARPE
            (can't believe his luck)
          You're a dream.

                  ANGELIQUE
          Almost. Close your eyes.
          Trust me.

Sharpe closes his eyes. Angelique presses her hand against the pillar and PUSHES THROUGH THE SOLID CONCRETE, the stone crumbling into grey dust around her probing hand.

ANGLE ON SHARPE, eyes still closed.

                    SHARPE
          Can I look now?

                  ANGELIQUE
          You can look now.

Sharpe opens his eyes.

Angelique is holding her hand out to him. Resting in her palm is the Box.

                  ANGELIQUE
          Time to play another
          game.

INT. MERCHANT'S APARTMENT, BEDROOM - NIGHT

John lies asleep. Bobbi is propped up, looking at him with a concerned expression.

John's faces twitches slightly and his eyes move in REM. Camera TRACKS into his face and DISSOLVES TO...

INT. LIVING ROOM, MID-1960'S - (JOHN'S DREAM-MEMORY)

A seven-year-old boy (JOHN) sits on the floor, sketching and cartooning on myriad pieces of paper.

Leaving a group of OTHER ADULTS, the grandmother from the earlier dream walks over to him. She looks at his drawings and GASPS. They are all childish and untutored renditions of Box designs and Cat's-Cradle designs.

CLOSE on Grandma's face, as from a child's POV.

> GRANDMOTHER
> You're the one, Johnny.
> The one they've been
> waiting for.

Suddenly, interrupting the dream like a startling and subconscious editing device, there is a DAZZLING BURST OF LIGHT like the dizzying lights of the lobby.

When we return, it is clearly another time. The room is sombre.

The CHILD'S POV CAMERA moves through many black-clad adults to reach...

...a coffin, laid out in the living room as in the European tradition of family wakes.

John's grandmother, dead, is in it. The POV peers into the coffin at her.

> 7-YEAR-OLD JOHN
> Grandma... You said you'd tell me. You said you'd explain...

Again, the DAZZLING LIGHTS jolt us — and we SMASH-CUT TO:

INT. MERCHANT'S APARTMENT, BEDROOM - NIGHT

John's eyes jerk open in panic. Before he can scream or cry out, Bobbi is there — stroking his brow, kissing his face, holding him.

> BOBBI
> Honey, I'm here. I'm here. It's okay.

> JOHN
> (half-whispered)
> Is it?

He moves into Bobbi's safe and comforting embrace, but his words seem to echo in the room.

INT. THE BUILDING, BASEMENT - NIGHT

Sharpe is sitting cross-legged on the floor, working the Box with intense concentration.

Angelique is behind him, rubbing his shoulders in encouragement.

> ANGELIQUE
> I have such sights to
> show you. Mysteries.
> Wonders...

The Box suddenly flies from Sharpe's hands and he watches in surprise as it completes its movements.

> SHARPE
> Now?

> ANGELIQUE
> Now.

Angelique straightens up and stands back...

WHOOOSH! The chains fly from the Box and rip into Sharpe's flesh as he SCREAMS in agony.

The basement is suddenly flooded in supernatural blue light and a space opens ahead of them, a shadowed space seeming to give onto vast regions beyond...

Emerging from the shadows comes PINHEAD, the Black Pope of HELLRAISER I, II & III, back-lit, stately but terrifying.

And he's not alone. SOMETHING prowls in the shadows behind Pinhead, pacing back and forth like a caged predator. Something big, vicious, and hungry. We can't see it clearly yet (and won't for another few scenes) but its barely glimpsed presence is horrifying enough.

> SHARPE
> No! No! What's happening?!!

Sharpe, wounded and bleeding, staggers to his feet, the chains from the Box ripping clear of his flesh. Does this mean he's going to get away?

No. Another chain flies from the shadows beyond, anchors itself viciously into Sharpe's neck, yanks him off his feet, and pulls him rapidly into the shadows.

His SCREAM mingles with the ROARS of the thing in the shadows...

...and then both are cut off abruptly as the space is re-sealed, leaving Pinhead alone with Angelique.

For a beat, they regard each other. Angelique looks both surprised and disappointed at the sight of Pinhead.

> ANGELIQUE
> Things seem to have changed. I was expecting my Clowns.

PINHEAD
Hell is more ordered since
your time, Princess. And
much less amusing.

His tone carries a hint of disapproval at this figure from Hell's past.

It's already clear that these two aren't going to like each other.

ANGELIQUE
I'm in favour of
efficiency, Demon. But I
can't abide dullness.

Pinhead looks around the pretty dull basement space.

PINHEAD
Then why are we here?

ANGELIQUE
Come with me.

CUT TO:

INT. THE BUILDING, LOBBY - NIGHT

Angelique and Pinhead are in the deserted lobby. Pinhead looks at the Box-like murals and then focuses on the back wall with its moving panel.

PINHEAD
The Box did this?

> ANGELIQUE
> A man did this — but the
> Box called him. Called to
> his blood.

Pinhead is hardly listening, lost in the movements of the panels as if waiting for something...

> ANGELIQUE
> His ancestor made the Box.
> And would have <u>un</u>made all
> of us. I killed him...

The panel moves into a new pattern. Pinhead stares, excited...

> ANGELIQUE
> ...but failed to kill his
> offspring. Now I fear his
> genius is reborn.

...as, for a brief moment, BLUE LIGHT crackles over the panel — and then disappears as the pattern moves on.

Pinhead looks at Angelique contemptuously.

> PINHEAD
> You've been away too
> long, Princess. Fear is
> for humans.

> ANGELIQUE
> Merchant must die before
> he proves you wrong.

> PINHEAD
> He'll die. But not yet. Imagine that panel frozen in the position of a moment ago. This isn't a room — it's a holocaust waiting to wake itself.

Angelique looks round the lobby.

> ANGELIQUE
> A Lament Configuration? On this scale?

> PINHEAD
> A vast and permanent gateway to the fields of human flesh.

> ANGELIQUE
> Using Merchant is playing with fire.

Pinhead raises an eyebrow.

> PINHEAD
> How entirely appropriate.

CUT TO:

EXT. MERCHANT'S DESIGN STUDIO - DAY

An old warehouse district yuppified into a design area. One of the buildings houses John's design studio.

DISSOLVE TO:

INT. MERCHANT'S STUDIO - DAY (CONT.)

A big open-plan loft-space with partitioned offices, the biggest of which is John's own.
Framed drawings, designs, and photographs cover the walls showing buildings and spaces John has worked on in the past as well as projects in development.

A thematic motif runs through every piece of work. In one way or another and to a greater or lesser extent, each design shows an influence from either the Lament Configuration or from Lemarchand's cat's-cradle design for the Box's opposite. It's as if John's gene-pool were speaking through his unconscious.

Framed on a wall in John's office is Lemarchand's design itself, the original document brought to America by Genevieve.

John is standing with his back to his door as AN ASSISTANT shows in a visitor and leaves.

> JOHN
> (turning)
> Take a seat, I'll be...

He stops, stunned, as he finds himself looking at Angelique. She holds his gaze. For a beat, it's almost as if he's in a trance-like state.

His voice is small and confused.

                    JOHN
            I... I know you...

Angelique crosses to him and holds out her
hand. He shakes it, blinking himself back
into something approaching normality.

                  ANGELIQUE
            You've no idea what a
            pleasure it is to meet
            you. Again.

                    JOHN
            You were there. Last
            night.

Angelique walks around the office, looking
at the designs.

                  ANGELIQUE
            Oh yes. This is all very
            good. You're the one
            we've been waiting for.

John reacts to this echo of the phrase
we've heard his grandmother say in his
dreams.

                    JOHN
            Who are you?

                  ANGELIQUE
            A friend, I hope. A
            client, I'm sure.

John stares at her as she reaches the
framed cat's-cradle design. For an all-
but-subliminal FLASH, she looks different

— her hair and makeup more like her 18th Century self.

Angelique takes a quick breath at the sight of the design as if there's something disturbing or dangerous about it.

>   ANGELIQUE
>   This is yours?
>
>   JOHN
>   No. It's been in the
>   family for centuries.
>   I'm... working on
>   something based on it.
>   I--
>
>   ANGELIQUE
>   (interrupting)
>   May I see it?
>
>   JOHN
>   Nobody's seen it.
>
>   ANGELIQUE
>   Then let me be the first.
>   It'll be our secret.

John — under the same kind of hypnotic sway his ancestor once was with this woman — clicks on the computer on his desk and a 3-D SIMULATION appears on the monitor.

It looks like an art-installation in a gallery space. The six faces of the Box are set at various angles.

                    JOHN
          Something I wanted to
          do with mirrors and
          lasers...

Angelique stares fascinated at the screen.

John stares fascinated at Angelique. Again, a FLASH or a BLURRING of this reality and the past. Very brief.

On the screen, BEAMS OF LIGHT suddenly burst from the six faces, echoing the lines drawn from the faces in the original design. The beams meet, merge, and reflect in the centre of the simulated space, coalescing into a beautiful LIGHT-SCULPTURE — which is a luminous 3-D echo of the cat's cradle.

The beams from the six faces blink off, leaving the luminescent cat's cradle hovering in the middle of the simulated room.

Angelique stares at it, fascinated and horrified.

                    JOHN
          See, in theory it's
          possible. Perpetual light.
          Trapped light feeding off
          its own reflections.

He clicks the monitor off.

                    JOHN
          But I could never make

> it work. I'd get a few
> seconds, then it'd blink
> out.

Angelique, visibly relieved at the disappearance of the image, walks away from the desk into the room.

> ANGELIQUE
> Sometimes a few seconds
> are more than enough,
> toymaker.

> JOHN
> What did you call me? Who
> *are* you?

> ANGELIQUE
> You think you don't
> remember. But your blood
> knows. Let it remind you.

And suddenly the image in front of John TRANSFORMS. Angelique remains precisely where she is, but she is dressed in the style of the 18th century and the room around her is not John's office but the ante chamber of the Chateau Du Reve.

John blinks and the image dissolves back to the present.

> JOHN
> (almost unconsciously)
> Angelique...

Angelique gives a delighted laugh. She smiles beguilingly.

                    ANGELIQUE
          You know me from dreams,
          John Merchant. John
          Lemarchand. We have a
          history together. We have
          a destiny together.

Angelique's manner is as hypnotically seductive as it was with Phillip centuries before, the room's lights fading around her. John has to fight a spinning head to answer.

                    JOHN
          I don't believe in
          destiny.

                    ANGELIQUE
          You think your work on
          the building was an
          accident? No. It called
          to you, John.

She crosses the room to him, her beautiful eyes never leaving his face. She strokes his cheek.

                    ANGELIQUE
          We have great work to do.
          I shall be in touch.

She turns and leaves, John staring after her, incredulous and fascinated.

EXT. THE BUILDING - EVENING

The building framed against a twilight

sky.

INT. THE BUILDING, TOP-FLOOR CORRIDOR - EVENING

An elevator door at the far end opens and VALERIE DYSON, a uniformed Security Officer, exits and walks up the corridor.

She's about 40 and is speaking into a cell-phone.

>   VALERIE
> I know, honey. I know.
> Homework's <u>always</u> sucked.
> And I <u>am</u> helping. See,
> you do the work and get
> the <u>grades</u>. And I walk
> round empty buildings
> and get the <u>money</u>. And,
> between us, we send you
> to college. You get it?
> It's teamwork.

To the CRACKLE of a replying child on the cell-phone, Valerie reaches a door to an office suite.

>   VALERIE
> Yeah. Yeah. Yeah. Listen,
> honey, I've gotta check
> on something. I'll see
> you later, okay? I love
> you.

She holsters the cell-phone and goes in.

INT. THE BUILDING, OFFICE-SUITE - EVENING (CONT.)

Valerie looks around the large room, puzzled. It's strangely-lit — a single pool of light near the front dissolving into shadows beyond. She exhales — and her breath is visible in the unnaturally chilly air. A single table is in the room. On it is the Box.

>VALERIE
>Hello?

From the shadows Angelique emerges into the little light. Valerie is instantly alert and on-guard.

>VALERIE
>Ma'am — the building is
>closed. And this office
>is vacant.

>ANGELIQUE
>Not anymore.

>VALERIE
>You've rented it?

>ANGELIQUE
>Arrangements have been
>made.

>VALERIE
>Well, I've heard nothing
>about it. I'll have to--

                    ANGELIQUE
                (interrupting)
            You'll have to leave. My
            colleague and I are in
            conference.

Colleague? Valerie looks deeper into the room...

In the far shadows, we suddenly sense another brooding presence. And sounds come faintly — disturbing sounds, like the rattling of chains.

Valerie looks back at Angelique, at the secret amusement on her face. The atmosphere is increasingly uncomfortable.

                    ANGELIQUE
            Perhaps we can deal with
            this tomorrow?

Valerie pauses, then nods her head nervously. Screw this. She's got a kid to get through school. She doesn't need any trouble. She backs out of the room...

INT. HOTEL CORRIDOR - EVENING (CONT.)

...closing the door in front of her. She turns and heads down to the elevator. Halfway, something makes her look back.

She GASPS. The area by the office-suite door is suddenly dark as if blackness is bleeding from the room into the corridor. And then she hears the sound of the door opening...

...and she's rushing to the elevator and hitting the button.

The elevator doors open and she runs in, only then turning to look back...

She SCREAMS. The BEAST that prowled in the shadows behind Pinhead earlier is in the corridor by the office door. Semi-human but four-legged, it's like something the scientists at Cenobite Central made as a joke from what was left of a man and what was left of a dog after a particularly nasty car crash.

Valerie jabs frantically at the first-floor button.

For a frozen second the Beast — whose eyes are only black pits and who locates its prey by smell and sound — 'stares' down the corridor at her.

Then it launches itself. Its speed is terrifying. Braying like a hyena, it hurtles impossibly forward defying all laws of gravity, running up and down the walls, across the ceiling, over the floor.

             VALERIE
        NO!! NOOOO!!!

At the very last second — just as the bestial face is inches from the open door, its teeth CHATTERING together at incredible speed (showing a distinct family resemblance to Pinhead's old ally The Chatterer, though at a horribly devolved level) — the elevator door slams shut.

INT. HOTEL ELEVATOR - EVENING (CONT.)

To the SOUND of the Beast scrabbling against the outer door, the elevator cabin begins to move downward.

> VALERIE
> Oh, thank God! Thank God!!

She looks at the floor display above the door. The electronic numerals show the passing floors: 7, 6, 5, 4, 3, 2.

Her panicked breathing finally slowing, she moves toward the door as her floor approaches...

...but the elevator does not stop. And the numbers keep descending: 1, 0, -1, -2, -3...

Her fingers stab repeatedly at the first-floor button.

> VALERIE
> Shit. C'mon. C'mon!

The numbers keep descending: -4, -5, -6...

Her finger reaches forward again...

...and suddenly the elevator's speed

increases horribly. Valerie is thrown from her feet as the cabin rockets downward.

The quiet hum of the lift machinery becomes A SCREECHING HOWL, and the LCD display is a scarlet BLUR of impossible numbers as the cabin speeds down... down... down...

And Valerie scrabbles at the walls, trying impossibly to clamber up them to avoid the inevitable crash.

And then the cabin stops. Stops suddenly and jarringly, but without the explosive bone-crushing finality we expected.

The howl of the machinery is over, the LCD a burn-out. And Valerie is in the centre of the cabin, frozen in shock but unharmed. Is it over?

Unfortunately not. The door starts to GLOW RED-HOT as if unbelievable furnaces burn somewhere just beyond its fragile protection...

...and HIDEOUS SOUNDS begin to drift in from outside — nightmarish sounds of indescribable agony and unspeakable joy growing in intensity and volume by the second.

I think we know where Valerie has landed, don't we?

The door PINGS as if to signal its arrival and its imminent opening. Which isn't something she's keen to see.

                    VALERIE
               Oh God. No. No!

She presses her hands on the door in a
terrified attempt to stop it from opening.

                    VALERIE
               AAAAAHHH!!!

She staggers back, SCREAMING in agony and
staring at her palms — which are HORRIBLY
BLISTERED.

There's nothing she can do — except to
stare in horror at the door and wait for
it to open...

...and the floor of the cabin gives way.
Splitting along the centre, it opens wide
in less then a second and Valerie drops
helplessly out of sight into the terrible
BLACK VOID below...

INT. BLACK VOID

ANGLE UPWARDS/VALERIE'S POV — Blackness
all around and the sense of dizzyingly
fast descent. Up above — and fast receding
— is the single square of light which is
the elevator cabin seen through its open
floor...

                    VALERIE
               NOOOOOOOO!!!!!

...Smaller and smaller grows this last
precious glimpse of light until suddenly

even it is cut off as the floor SLAMS back into place and all is darkness and terror.

INT. THE BUILDING, OFFICE SUITE – EVENING

Angelique and Pinhead stand in the shadows. Somewhere beyond them, we hear the impatient prowling of the Beast.

> PINHEAD
> Where is Merchant?

> ANGELIQUE
> All but in my grasp.

Pinhead sneers in dismissive impatience.

> PINHEAD
> I'd have what was left of
> his mouth begging to work
> for us by now!

> ANGELIQUE
> Your Hell has forgotten
> not only chaos and
> laughter but the slow
> delight of temptation.

> PINHEAD
> I've harvested more souls
> than you could dream of
> and their suffering is
> with me always. That is a
> slow delight.

Angelique turns angrily and heads for the

door. Pinhead speaks back to her.

>   PINHEAD
>   Your methods are outmoded,
>   Angelique. Hell is _mine_.
>   Adjust, or--

Angelique turns back in the open door and interrupts.

>   ANGELIQUE
>   I will have Merchant!

She exits...

INT. THE BUILDING, TOP-FLOOR CORRIDOR (CONT.)

...and slams the door behind her. She walks away.

>   ANGELIQUE
>   (to herself)
>   And I will have Hell. _My_
>   Hell!

INT. THE BUILDING, OFFICE-SUITE - EVENING

Pinhead looks at the closed door, amused. He steps further forward into the room and stands, concentrating.

Slowly, supernaturally, the space around him changes in nature.

The light alters, the shadows shift...

The room feels like A CHAMBER OF HELL, a place whose shadows seem to give on to unseen vistas from where terrible SOUNDS emanate.

The Beast prowls the perimeters of the room. Other CENOBITES are half-glimpsed in the blue shadows.

Like a general addressing his troops or the Pope bringing his Cardinals up to speed, Pinhead addresses them.

> PINHEAD
> I grow impatient with
> the Princess. Human
> acquiescence is obtained
> as easily by terror as by
> temptation...

CUT TO:

INT. THE BUILDING, LOBBY- EVENING

Angelique walks through the deserted lobby. She pauses in the centre and looks up at the back wall's moving panel.

Then her eyes flick from corner to corner of the room, from face to face of the huge Box-like murals, and back to the centre of the room as if judging angles, judging distances...

We see her mind work. She's seeing something

here, something that Pinhead knows nothing
about...

> CUT TO:

INT. MERCHANT'S APARTMENT, BEDROOM - NIGHT

TRACK into John's dreaming face.

> DISSOLVE TO:

DREAMSPACE

- The SIMULATED LIGHT-SCULPTURE we saw on his computer spins, free-floating against a dream-like one-coloured background.
- His Grandmother's face.

> GRANDMOTHER
> You're the one they've been waiting for.

- Angelique's face.

> ANGELIQUE
> You're the one we've been waiting for.

EXT. THE BUILDING, FORECOURT - (THAT MOMENT)

CLOSE on Angelique standing in the night.

CLOSER still on her eyes, narrowing in concentration as if projecting thoughts...

DREAMSCAPE

- Angelique and John, naked and entwined, making love. John is sexually aggressive, his hands twisted tight in her hair. Angelique's voice ECHOES over and over.

> ANGELIQUE
> Whatever you want...
> Whatever you want...
> Whatever you want...

- The camera PANS from the lovers to find an 18th century AUTOMATON (like those Lemarchand made): A beautiful woman who curtseys and bows her head. As she lifts it again, the face is suddenly TERRIFYING and DEMONIC.

A jarring, startling RINGING SOUND.

INT. MERCHANT'S APARTMENT, BEDROOM - DAWN

The ringing is the bedside phone.

John blinks awake in shock and grabs at the phone as Bobbi peers at him from sleepy eyes.

> BOBBI
> What time is it? Who the
> hell is that?

                    JOHN
               (into phone)
          Hello?

                    ANGELIQUE
               (on phone)
          Good morning, toymaker.

John spins half-out of bed to sit on the side, pressing the phone tight to his ear.

Bobbi, left back on her side of the bed and excluded from the call, stares at John's back, troubled.

We can now only hear John's half of the conversation, which gives nothing away.

                    JOHN
               (ad-lib)
          Yeah... Uh-huh... OK...
               (etc.)

John replaces the phone and turns back to Bobbi's curious eyes.

                    JOHN
          A client. He's Japanese.
          No sense of time.
          Business, business.

He reaches over and strokes Bobbi's brow.

                    JOHN
          Go back to sleep. It's
          early.

Each lies on their side away from each

other. And each keeps their eyes open —
Bobbi's worried, John's guilty, troubled.

EXT. WAREHOUSE/DESIGN DISTRICT - DAY

The area of town that houses John's business.

ANGLE ON a warehouse converted to an Art Gallery.

> DISSOLVE TO:

INT. ART GALLERY - DAY

A few CUSTOMERS weave in and out of the various alcoves and rooms within the huge ground-floor space.

John stands in front of a large canvas. He senses a presence nearby and turns. It's Angelique. They smile in greeting.

> JOHN
> I don't know why I'm here.

> ANGELIQUE
> Yes you do.

Her eyes lock on his. Her gaze is challenging and inviting.

John stares at her, lost in her beauty, her sexuality, her blatant availability.

                    ANGELIQUE
            Whatever you want...

John reacts to this echo from his erotic dream. She smiles.

                    ANGELIQUE
            Were we good together?

A beat.
                    JOHN
            Yes.

                    ANGELIQUE
            I knew we would be. I've
            always known.

She takes his arm and leads him further into the gallery.

INT. MERCHANT'S APARTMENT - DAY

Bobbi, supporting an over-filled laundry basket, is at the apartment door talking to Jack, who is on the floor working on a model kit with profound seriousness.

                    BOBBI
            Mommy'll be five minutes,
            honey. Okay?

                    JACK
            (eyes not leaving his kit)
            Shh, mom. I'm
            concentrating.

Bobbi grins and maneuvers herself out of

the apartment.

INT. LAUNDRY CORRIDOR - DAY

A NEON LIGHT FLICKERS on the ceiling. Another's dead. There's an oppressive silence as Bobbi walks towards the laundry room.

A SHARP NOISE. She spins round. The detergent on top of the clothes topples. She grabs it. There's nothing behind her.

But an atmosphere of foreboding remains as she reaches the laundry room. She casts another glance down the corridor as she goes in. Nothing, just the flicker and the silence.

INT. LAUNDRY ROOM - DAY (CONT.)

The laundry room — a bank of washing machine, a table, couple of plastic chairs, and a bank of dryers — is empty.

But as Bobbi goes through the routine — opening two washers, loading them, counting her quarters, sprinkling the powder — the creepy atmosphere that we felt in the corridor continues.

Suddenly — THWAP! THWAP! THWAP! — a terrible beating sound fills the air. Bobbie jumps and cries out. What is it?

Through the window, we see a PIGEON. The

sound is merely its wings beating against the glass. It flies off.

Bobbi sighs and continues. But the edgy atmosphere remains. We feel as if there's a presence on the edges of our senses, something watching and waiting. Something malign.

Perhaps it's the shadows in the room. Do they move at the corner of our vision? The feeling persists.

A sense of imminence. Something is going to happen. Something bad.
Bobbi hits the start button and straightens up. She glances round the room again. Nothing. She's being silly. And then she glances upwards, as if thinking. Suddenly she's certain...

> BOBBI
> (fearful whisper)
> Jack...

...and she's gone. Ignoring the basket, she's out the room.

INT. LAUNDRY ROOM CORRIDOR - DAY (CONT.)

The neon flickers as Bobbi runs to the door to the stairs...

INT. STAIRS BETWEEN FLOORS - DAY (CONT.)

...and hurtles up the one flight to their

apartment floor.

SOUNDS SWELL on the soundtrack — a BANGING like an angry fist on an apartment wall and a MUFFLED VOICE raised in anger. And something else.

A LOW HELLISH RUMBLING on the very edge of perception — like a distant echo of unimaginable machines, indescribably vast and inexpressibly malicious.

Bobbi heaves open the door to their corridor, runs out...

INT. CORRIDOR TO MERCHANT'S APARTMENT - DAY (CONT.)

...and suddenly slows, staring ahead, her face appalled.

Pulsing SHAFTS OF BLUE LIGHT are visible beneath and behind the apartment door. The LOW RUMBLES are louder now.

Something has come to her home. And it's behind her door. With her child.

Further down the corridor, the THUMPING continues.

> ELDERLY NEIGHBOUR
> (off)
> Stop it! Be quiet! I've
> called the Police! (etc.,
> ad-lib)

Bobbi runs to her door, no thought for her own safety...

                    BOBBI
          Jack!

...only that of her child. She opens the door.

INT. MERCHANTS' APARTMENT - DAY (CONT.)

The front room's empty. Jack's model kit lies crushed on the floor. The BLUE LIGHT comes from the open door to the next room.

                    BOBBI
          Jack? Jack!!

Terror mounting, the Blue Light playing across her face, Bobbi heads for the other room...

Only to stop as Jack walks out into the doorway. Bobbi doesn't take time to notice the strange, stunned look on his face.

                    BOBBI
          Jack! Thank God. Come
          here.

                    JACK
          I can't, mommy. He won't
          let me.

One of Jack's arms is stretched out back into the room and, as Bobbi moves forward and the angle changes, we see why.

Pinhead is holding the boy's hand.

Bobbi SCREAMS as the demon smiles cruelly at her.

>   BOBBI
> Get your hands off him!

>   PINHEAD
> Young. Unformed. What
> appetites I could teach
> him. What endless hungers
> he could learn.

Bobbi rushes forward. Pinhead jabs a forbidding finger.

>   PINHEAD
> Stay!

>   BOBBI
> Give him to me!! Please,
> please!!

>   PINHEAD
> You suffer beautifully.
> But we're here for
> business, not pleasure.

>   BOBBI
> What?! Just tell me what
> you want!!

Pinhead looks from her to Jack and back. He smiles.

>   PINHEAD
> I want bait. Live bait.

FADE TO BLACK

INT. ART GALLERY - DAY

Angelique and John walk into a partitioned space in the gallery. It houses some large video-installation and, apart from the light from the bank of monitors, is dark.

There is a single viewing bench. Nobody is in there.

Angelique pauses and looks up at John. She's waiting.

> JOHN
> (trying to stay rational)
> I've dreamed of you. Not just last night. For years. But... But when I wake up, it's Bobbi who's there. Bobbi.

Angelique says nothing, does nothing. She's still waiting.

John blinks, as if fighting a powerful spell. With each blink, a FLASH IMAGE — The Box, The Cat's-Cradle, Grandma, Bobbi...

But it's no good. The spell is too strong. He leans down, and they kiss. Their arms wrap around each other slowly and they press their bodies together in a passionate embrace.

Still kissing, they sink onto the bench.

Their hands roam each other's bodies. John lowers his head, kissing her neck and shoulders. She puts her hands to the back of his head, pushing him lower. He kisses her breast wildly. Encouraged by her moans, he slips his hand beneath her skirt.

Angelique's head is thrown back in pleasure. It's clear that this is not just Hellish seduction. She's getting off on it too. Her eyes half-close, her mouth half-opens...

...and something else begins to happen. Her guard down, her blood inflamed, her passion pulsing, she begins unknowingly to slip her mask of humanity.

It's subtle at first, a strange de-focused effect that blurs her features as her face begins to twitch in more than passion.

Carried away by John's intimate caresses, she is moving into a pre-orgasmic state, her breathing heavy and animal-like. John raises his head, his hand still lost between her legs...

...and GASPS in shock as he looks at her face.

Angelique's eyes are SOLID MASSES OF GLISTENING BLACKNESS.

JOHN
My God!

He leaps to his feet in shock and fear, backing away.

Angelique, ecstasy turned to frustration and rage, throws back her head and roars. Her mouth is FANGED and DEMONIC.

Realising what she looks like, Angelique waves an arm at the bank of monitors and they BLOW OUT en masse, plunging the room into shadowed darkness.

John turns and runs, fleeing the partitioned space as Angelique's transformation climaxes in the darkness, giving us a shadowed sense of her terrible appearance. John flees through the rest of the gallery — stared at strangely by the other CUSTOMERS.

EXT. APARTMENT BUILDING - DUSK

It's later. Night is falling as John's car pulls up and John gets out and runs to the building.

INT. APARTMENT BUILDING CORRIDOR - NIGHT

John moves down the corridor — and freezes.

The door to John's apartment has across it a series of yellow tapes with black letters spelling out CRIME SCENE DO NOT CROSS.

> JOHN
> Oh Christ.

He rushes forward and opens the door, ripping the tape aside.

> JOHN
> Bobbi?! Jack?!!

INT. MERCHANT'S APARTMENT - NIGHT (CONT.)

John rushes round the apartment.

No signs of disturbance. But no Bobbi. And no Jack. He cries out to the empty room...

> JOHN
> What happened?! What happened?!!

His eyes go to the back of the front door.

Tacked to it is the ripped-off magazine cover featuring his building.

> GRANDMOTHER (O.S.)
> (echoed, ghostly)
> You're the one they've been waiting for.

As he looks at it, the whole cover suddenly begins to POUR WITH BLOOD.

John gets the message.

INT. BUILDING, TOP-FLOOR OFFICE-SUITE – NIGHT

Bobbi and Jack crouch on the floor of the office, their breaths visible in the supernaturally cold air. Bobbi hugs Jack protectively in the pool of light, while in the threatening shadows beyond, we hear the padding and the prowling of the half-seen circling Beast which guards them.

The Box still sits on the table. Jack points at it.

> JACK
> Look, Mommy. Like Daddy's drawings.

Bobbi stares at the Box. Jack's right. She reaches out and picks it up. In the background, the Beast raises its blind head. What's happening?

Bobbi runs her hand over the Box like so many before her and, like so many before her, her fingers almost instinctively find the appropriate movements.

Her thumb strokes the central circle-motif and there is the TINIEST FLASH OF BLUE LIGHT...

...and the Beast steps menacingly forward, SNARLING.

Bobbi drops the Box and cradles the terrified Jack.

EXT. THE BUILDING - NIGHT

The building framed against a night sky in which razor-thin clouds slice across a huge and heavy moon.

John runs across the forecourt and through the entrance.

INT. THE BUILDING, LOBBY - NIGHT (CONT.)

John stands in the deserted lobby.

>   JOHN
> Bobbi! Bobbi!!

His voice echoes in the empty reaches of the place. He runs through it until his eye is caught by the elevator — where the number 7 is flashing on and off on the indicator above it.

                                TIME-CUT TO:

INT. THE BUILDING, TOP-FLOOR CORRIDOR - NIGHT

John exits the elevator and stares down the long corridor.

JOHN'S POV — the whole corridor has become Hellish. We stare down a nightmarish gauntlet, a creepy, cold, shadowed walkway in which chains and hooks hang and rattle. The floor is wet and mildewed, the doors warped and slimy. At the far end, beckoning

BLUE LIGHT pulses from the door of the office-suite.

Horrible LOW SOUNDS fill the air, like the laboured breathing of some vast asthmatic creature, as John begins to make his way cautious way down.

As his feet pass a door, BLOOD oozes in rich quantities from beneath it.

A TERRIBLE CACKLING LAUGH. From nowhere. From everywhere.

A chain shivers and twists, spinning to reveal a BABY'S LIVER skewered on a hook.

CLOSE on John's feet — as a SLITHERING BLACK EEL writhes over them to disappear into the shadows.

In a web on a wall, A PREGNANT SPIDER bursts into labour and SCORES OF TINY SPIDERS spill from her body, rushing everywhere.

John moves resolutely on despite all these horrors, drawing nearer to the office-suite and the near-blinding BLUE LIGHT.

He reaches the door...

                    JOHN
  Bobbi? Jack?

...and walks, dazzled and half-blinded, into the light.

INT. THE BUILDING, TOP-FLOOR OFFICE-SUITE - NIGHT (CONT.)

For a moment, all John can see is the intense Blue Light. Then it resolves. Ahead of John, still on the floor, are Bobbi and Jack. John starts to rush forward...

                  JOHN
    Thank God!

...and suddenly the Beast springs forward from the shadows, stopping close to Bobbi and Jack, glaring at John.

                  BOBBI
    John, don't!

John staggers to a halt, shocked and scared.

                  JOHN
    What the...

The Beast comes no nearer. But Pinhead now emerges from the shadows also. He smiles at John.

                  JOHN
    I don't know who or what
    you are and I don't care.
    I just want my wife. I
    just want my son.

                  PINHEAD
    I understand. You love
    this boy. You have plans
    for him. Hopes and

dreams. A whole imagined
future where you love him
and watch him grow.

                    JOHN
              (helpless truth)
Yes.

                  PINHEAD
Then first you must
complete your work. Or,
though the child will not
die here, for a thousand
years his dearest wish
will be that he had.

                    JOHN
For God's sake, how can
you—(be so cruel?)

                  PINHEAD
              (interrupting)
Do I look like someone
who cares what <u>God</u>
thinks?

                    JOHN
Just tell me what you
want.

                  PINHEAD
         (gestures at table)
Look at that Box. A
pathway to Hell made by
an ancestor of yours.

Both John and Bobbi stare at the Box and
then at each other.

John's dreams. His Grandmother's claims. Not so crazy.

> PINHEAD
> The panel downstairs? Potentially a bigger pathway. You will help it fulfil its promise.

> BOBBI
> John. Your dreams. Your grandmother. It's all true. All true. You mustn't do this. You can't let more of these things into the world!

Pinhead's mocking laughter rings out as John looks at his wife and child, at the monsters beside them.

> JOHN
> Bobbi —right now you and Jack are all the world I care about. I have to do this.

TIME-CUT TO:

INT. TOP-FLOOR CORRIDOR - NIGHT

John, Bobbi and Jack walk down the corridor passing the many doors on the way to the elevator, Pinhead behind them.

As they draw abreast another door John suddenly jumps sideways, knocking Bobbi and Jack through the door ahead of him.

INT. THE BUILDING, STAIRWELL - NIGHT (CONT.)

As Bobbi steadies Hack, John slams the door closed, yanking down the bar-lock.

A HOOKED CHAIN instantly splinters through the wood!

> JOHN
> Go! Go!!

The three of them pelt down the stairwell to the SOUND of the door smashing above them.

They reach the next level and exit through the door.

INT. THE BUILDING, NEXT FLOOR CORRIDOR - NIGHT (CONT.)

John glances up and down the corridor.

> JOHN
> Bobbi — that way! Another staircase!

Bobbi hugs jack fiercely and runs the way John pointed.

John grabs Jack and rushes him to the elevator door. He hits the button, glancing anxiously back at the stairwell door.

The elevator opens and John places Jack inside. Jack, scared, reaches for his dad.

> JOHN
> No, Jack. The lobby. I'll
> meet you there. Be brave.
> Be good.

The door closes. John turns back to face the corridor.

> JOHN
> C'mon, you bastard. It's
> me you want.

The stairwell door bursts open, and Pinhead comes through.

John pauses just long enough to let the demon catch sight of him and then he disappears down an intersecting corridor.

INT. THE BUILDING, OTHER CORRIDOR - (CONT.)

John runs madly toward another door which he slams open, revealing another stairwell which he rushes down.

INT. THE BUILDING, ANOTHER STAIRWELL

Bobbi is rushing down a different stairwell.

Below her, a rushing padding sound and the ROAR of the Beast.

                    BOBBI
            No! That's impossible!!

Apparently not. She turns round and runs up, terror-stricken, reaching the door to the top floor and smashing it open.

INT. TOP-FLOOR CORRIDOR (CONT.)

Bobbi runs down the corridor, glances over her shoulder...

The Beast bursts onto the floor, howling for blood, its speed terrifying, its appearance worse.

SCREAMING, Bobbi pushes open the door of the office-suite...

INT. TOP-FLOOR OFFICE-SUITE (CONT.)

...and slams it behind her.

She shoves the table up against the door and stands back, looking round helplessly.

SLAM!! The Beast smashes against the door from the other side.

The impact sends the Box careering down the table toward Bobbi.

SLAM!! It hits again. The door begins to splinter.

Bobbi's eyes flick from the Box to the

door and back. She snatches up the Box...

...just as the Beast comes smashing through the door to land on the table and rush down its length toward her.

Bobbi holds the Box up in front of her...

...and the Beast stops. Still terrifying, still powerful, but now it waits, hesitant.

> BOBBI
> Does this pathway work
> both ways?

Her fingers work feverishly at the Box. It starts to move...

...and the Beast, baring its teeth in a blood-curdling HOWL, leaps forward, hurtling through the air in attack-mode...

> CUT TO:

INT. THE BUILDING, LOBBY - NIGHT

John bursts into the lobby from a stairwell door and rushes over to the elevator.

A look of dread comes over him as he sees the elevator door banging constantly against the side of its doorjamb as if it is trying to open and something is wrong with the mechanism.
John runs to it... and it suddenly flies open with a terrifyingly LOUD NOISE.

John jumps in shock but moves further and looks in...

...and down. There is no cabin there, just a dizzying drop into blackness.

Incredibly distant, but disturbing, SOUNDS echo up the shaft. Sounds of flame, machinery, and agony.

                JOHN
   No! Jack! Jack!!

He hears a sound behind him and turns — to see Jack...

...and Angelique, back in human form, her hands resting on Jack's young shoulders. Her eyes are no longer seductive as they stare at John but cold and angry.

She looks down at Jack and coos like a nightmare vision of dark motherhood.

              ANGELIQUE
   So young. So tender. So
   ripe.

              JOHN
   Get your hands off him!

              ANGELIQUE
   Get your hands on the
   console, toymaker. You
   have work to do.

                          TIME-CUT TO:

John at the lectern, Angelique nearby still holding Jack.

> ANGELIQUE
> My colleague told you
> what to do?

> JOHN
> Yes.

He's working at the console, looking up at the patterns on the back wall panel, trying to find the infernal one.

> ANGELIQUE
> Don't.

> JOHN
> What?

> ANGELIQUE
> Don't do what he said.
> Make the Elysium
> Configuration instead.

John, genuinely confused, looks at Angelique but, before she can elucidate, Pinhead appears at the far end of the lobby.

Pinhead is grinning in triumph. He walks towards them. As he reaches the centre, Angelique speaks to John.

> ANGELIQUE
> The toymaker's design!
> The lights! I know
> they're here.

John looks rapidly from her to the walls, to the corners, to the reflective points on the surfaces and then keys an entry into the console.

His finger hovers over the 'enter' key. He looks at her. Why should he do what she wants? She raises a hand toward Jack's neck in threat.

                    ANGELIQUE
          Do it!!

John hits the key.

LIGHT-BEAMS shoot out from points in the wall faces, jetting in toward the centre of the lobby.

A sudden wave of suspicion washes over Pinhead's face.

The BEAMS meet, EXPLODING into a DAZZLING CORUSCATION.

Angelique, stepping well back to near the lectern and away from what's happening, grins in double-cross victory.

Pinhead ROARS in anger and fear. Suddenly, he tips his head way back — and a CHAIN flies from out of his mouth, jetting up straight toward the ceiling.

The hooked chain anchors itself into the ceiling — and PINHEAD flies upward along it at incredible speed, like a spider sucking itself back up a web-strand.

                    ANGELIQUE
          NOOOO!!!

Pinhead, fastened supernaturally to the ceiling like a humanoid insect, looks down...

...as the LIGHT-SCULPTURE from John's simulation of Lemarchand's cat's-cradle bursts into being far below him!

Pinhead, snarling in angry revenge, shoots his head in various directions as if summoning supernatural aid...

...and a MULTITUDE OF CHAINS suddenly fly from low angles and wrap themselves around Angelique, pirouetting rapidly up her body to cocoon her.

Simultaneously, as in the simulation, the original beams go off and the light-sculpture is left free-floating.

Jack — almost literally squeezed from Angelique's grasp as the chains fly upwards — is sent tumbling towards his father who grabs him protectively as...

...Angelique is yanked off her feet and pulled inexorably toward the centre of the room and the luminescent cat's-cradle.

From Pinhead's POV, Angelique disappears beneath the light.

                    ANGELIQUE
          It burns!! It burns!!!

John hugs Jack tightly to him.

                    JOHN
               (to himself)
      A few seconds is the best
      I ever got...

And, as if on cue, the cat's-cradle winks out of existence.

From this angle, we see that Angelique hadn't quite reached it and is lying still on the floor wrapped in the chains.

Pinhead lowers himself rapidly down and stalks toward John. As he passes Angelique, she raises her head and laughs hysterically as if driven mad by her proximity to destruction.

                  PINHEAD
               (to John)
      You're as dangerous as
      she said you were. No
      more games.

Pinhead flicks his head toward little Jack — and a hooked chain comes flying at the boy!

John launches himself forward, shoving Jack aside...

                  JOHN
          Run, Jack! Run!!

...and taking his place as the chain snaps viciously through the air...

...and slams right through John's throat, killing him instantly.

Jack is running across the lobby.

>   ANGELIQUE
> The bloodline! Kill it!!

Pinhead swings round, getting Jack in his eye-line...

...and Jack is suddenly grasped by an arm and pulled tight to a cradling body.

It's Bobbi — and she's got the Box in her hand. Straightening up and shielding Jack, she holds the Box forward, moving it.

>   BOBBI
> Go play with your dog,
> you bastard!

The Box flies from her hand, spinning and turning through its positions, and hits the floor.

>   PINHEAD
> No!!

The Box clicks into place...

...and Pinhead and Angelique are SUCKED into it, screaming their frustrated rage.

Bobbi pulls Jack tight to her and crouches down...

...as the whole lobby begins to SHAKE and

SHUDDER. EXPLOSIONS of LIGHT and SOUND fill the frame as Hell reclaims everything of its own: The Box is still open — and it's pulling the walls and murals into itself.

Suddenly — with a final explosive WHITE-OUT — all is silent and still and Bobbi and Jack are alone in the denuded and devastated lobby with the closed Box.

CLOSE on the Box.

TRACK OUT...

INT. MERCHANT'S APARTMENT - DAY

...to reveal the Box sitting on a table in the apartment.

Bobbi is sitting with Jack, talking to him.

> BOBBI
> The Box has to stay in our family, Jack. It must never get away from us. And it must never be opened. Never. We can't even destroy it until we know it's safe.

As Bobbi talks, the camera TRACKS in on Jack's completely attentive face as he absorbs what his mother is saying.

BOBBI
Your dad didn't know the
whole story. Neither do
I. But we're going to
find out, sweetheart.
I'll help you.

CLOSER and CLOSER to Jack's face, until his eye fills the frame...

BOBBI
You'll grow up knowing
everything. And so will
your children. And their
children.

...and we fall into the BLACKNESS of his pupil in EXTREME CLOSE UP...

BOBBI
And one day our family
will be ready...

COMPLETE BLACKNESS

BOBBI
Ready to put things
right...

We PAN along the blackness and suddenly, startlingly, tiny points of light appear. Distant STARS. We're in outer space.

BOBBI
...in a time yet to come.

Bobbi's last words echo over this transition, as...

EXT. DEEP SPACE

...A PASSENGER SHUTTLE suddenly hurtles toward us through the dark and silent void.

As it fills the frame, CUT TO REVERSE —

- and the shuttle speeds away from us, disappearing into the distant darkness.

Over its movement, a Super-imposed TITLE:

THE GOVERNMENT SHIP ENDEAVOUR VII
EN ROUTE TO THE SPACE STATION MINOS
2204AD

EXT. DEEP SPACE, MINOS

A different sector of space. TRACK down to reveal the TOWERS of the space station MINOS.

The Minos is an <u>ASTEROID</u>. For the most part craggy, barren and crater-studded, the top part is architectured — its towers and buildings laser-hewn from the solid rock.

LIGHTS shine from the towers.

TRACK in to one and DISSOLVE TO:

INT. PAUL'S CABIN/HOLDING PEN ANNEXE, MINOS

We're in a room decorated in 18th century

style and full of 18th century objects —
including one of Lemarchand's automata.

As the camera explores the room, A TV
broadcast plays in the BACKGROUND showing
news footage of a MASSIVE FIRE.

> TV ANNOUNCER (V.O.)
> Fires burn unchecked in
> the forests of Luna One
> tonight, roaring wildly
> beneath the great meta-
> glass canopies of the
> Pan-Pacific colony.
> Economic cutbacks that
> did away with the Suits-
> for-Settlers program are
> now being blamed for
> the colony's inability
> to simply turn off the
> air and thus douse the
> fire. Angry voices are
> being raised in Tokyo
> — particularly because
> Colonists could be
> transported to the Minos
> space station if that
> trillion-dollar facility
> was not a year behind
> schedule and, according
> to unconfirmed sources,
> not only out of radio-
> contact but also out of
> its geo-stationary orbit.
> (etc etc)

At this point, the TV clicks off and the
camera finds DR PAUL MERCHANT, sitting in

a Rocco-style chair.

Paul is identical to Phillip and John except for a mole on his cheek and his hair-colour. His face is haunted and obsessive. The single-minded genius of his ancestors has reached a neurotic fruition in him.

Behind him, we see on a wall the 2204 ad equivalent of a cork-board — a screen on which IMAGES replay in rotational display. The images are all familiar to us and all connected with the bloodline's history; The Box, the Cat's-cradle design, family portraits (photos of John, oils of Phillip, etc), sketches of demons (Pinhead and Angelique), The Building, etc etc.

Paul is addressing an unseen listener.

> PAUL
> The distance from all inhabited planets and colonies is important. It's unclear what effect on the space-time continuum such a surge of metaphysical energy will have.

There's something strange about his voice. A little un-human. A little computer-generated.

WIDEN TO REVEAL, sitting opposite him, his hand at a computer console on his lap, DR PAUL MERCHANT.

                    PAUL
                (The Real One)
            I have to assume we're
            far enough out now. Time
            has become a factor.

He hits a key on his console and the first
Paul BLINKS OUT of existence. He was a
holographic Computer Program.

Paul stands and crosses the room, and we
CHANGE ANGLE to see...

...that the other end of the room is very
different. The first part we saw was Paul's
living quarters. This part looks like a
control booth or a mixing bay. On a desk
are three 23rd century MONITORS and a pair
of latex gloves, each fingertip connected
by micro-filaments to a console beneath
one of the monitors.

Below the desk and the monitors is a
STAIRCASE leading down to a separate
structure — a large and massively solid
HOLDING PEN. It has a REINFORCED STEEL
DOOR with a large locking mechanism.

Paul sits at the desk and (as if movement-
sensitive) one of the monitors winks into
life, and we CUT TO...

INT. HOLDING PEN, MINOS (CONT.)

...a wall-mounted closed-circuit camera.
A red light clicks on to establish its
link with the monitor Paul is working.

The closed-circuit camera moves as if selecting an image area.

We PULL AWAY to take in the room. It is a large bare space, the walls massively thick and very tall. It is some kind of holding pen for something very dangerous. Currently, it's empty except for a shadowed figure cross-legged in a corner...

There's something familiar about this image. It's a posture we recognise. It reminds us of Elliot Spenser in HELLBOUND. It is a simple SERVO-ROBOT — a steel skeleton with fully articulated limbs. Its hands are close together in front of its chest.

And it's holding the Lament Configuration.

INT. PAUL'S CABIN/HOLDING PEN ANNEXE, MINOS (CONT.)

On the monitor, we see the same image of the robot and the Box.

Paul reaches over to the gloves...

...and a second monitor SQUAWKS into life, startling us.

On the monitor, CORRINNE COTTON, mid-20's and attractive, though her onepiece worksuit and business-like haircut do their best to ignore this. She's the administrator of the Minos.

                    CORINNE
                 (on monitor)
            Paul? Paul! I'm tracking
            a shuttle. It has to
            be government. They're
            coming. I'm serious.

A grimace of angry frustration crosses Paul's face.

                    PAUL
            Corinne, I can't be
            interrupted! Not now. <u>I'm</u>
            serious.

                    CORINNE
            Well, whatever it is
            you're doing, Paul, you
            better do it fast!

INT. SATELLITE-CONTROL/UTILITIES COMPLES, MINOS (CONT.)

Corrinne, too, is at a desk, working in front of a batch of monitors. Six of them show EXTERIOR SHOTS of HUGE FLAT PANELS, all decorated with Box-like patterns and all studded with (unlit) LIGHTS and MIRRORS. One monitor shows text: complicated co-ordinates for the alignment of the satellites.

                    PAUL
                 (on monitor)
            You too. How's it coming?

                    CORRINNE
            Slowly. You sure I can't

                    suit-up and nudge these
                    mothers by hand?

                              PAUL
                    You've got a good eye,
                    Corrinne, but the
                    alignment's too precise.
                    Trust the computers.
                    Just keep feeding in the
                    co-ordinates. We're so
                    close. We've got to do
                    it.

                              CORRINNE
                    Okay.

                                              CUT TO:

INT. PAUL'S CABIN/HOLDING PEN ANNEXE, MINOS (CONT)

Paul breaks the video-link. He looks to the third monitor. On the screen comes a high-definition image of the Lament Configuration. It changes to a skeletal 3-D rendering of the Box and moves around, showing it from all angles. The other monitor still shows the robot and the Box.

Breathing nervously, Paul squeezes his hands into the latex sensor-gloves.

Watching both the 3-D graphic and the image from within the pen, Paul moves his hands in front of him. He's not actually holding anything, but the movements of his hands look familiar.

On the micro-glass monitor, the image of the Box moves and changes as if Paul were actually moving a real Box.

We register the micro-filaments going into the console from the gloves before we CUT TO...

INT. HOLDING PEN, MINOS (CONT.)

...similar micro-filaments emerging from the wall behind the cross-legged robot and entering it at the elbows.

The skeletal steel hands of the robot begin to move. With remote-controlled precision, its metal fingers play over the Box, finding its secrets, discovering its hidden alignments, moving it closer and closer towards its final configuration...

...and the Box jumps from the robot's grip to land on the floor in front of it, where it makes its own final adjustment.

A beat of silence and stillness...

And the robot suddenly EXPLODES. In a jolting shock-moment, it is blasted apart, shattered to tiny fragments.

                                              CUT TO:

EXT. DEEP SPACE

The passenger shuttle Endeavour VII speeds

through space...

...and the camera SHIFTS ANGLE to REVEAL where it's heading...

EXT. MINOS, DEEP SPACE (CONT.)

...The Minos. In orbit around it are the SX SATELLITES, surrounding it in a way reminiscent of how the six faces of the Box were laid out by Lemarchand on the edge of his cat's-cradle design.

INT. PAUL'S CABIN, HOLDING PEN ANNEXE, MINOS

Corrinne enters the annex. Paul is at the desk, his back to her.

He's slumped back in his chair.

>   CORINNE
> Paul — I can't do it.
> It's your program. It
> needs you.

There's no reply.

>   CORINNE
> Paul? Paul, are you okay?

She moves round to him.

Paul looks like he's in shock. He doesn't even look at her.

                    CORINNE
          What's happened?

Suddenly — a MASSIVE BANGING beyond the steel-reinforced door, like something huge and angry is trying to get out.

Corinne starts in frightened shock.

                    CORINNE
          My God, Paul! What's
          happened?!

                    PAUL
          They're here. A whole
          lifetime — many lifetimes
          — to get ready... But the
          sight of them...

                    CORINNE
          Sight of who? Who's here?

Paul looks to the Pen-monitor. It clicks into life...

...and the snarling, terrifying face of the Chatterer-Beast fills the screen, accompanied by its heart-stopping ROAR.

                    CORINNE
          God in heaven, Paul. What
          have you done?

                                              CUT TO:

INT. HOLDING PEN, MINOS - THAT MOMENT

The Pen is transformed into a vision of Hell. A cold blue place of deep shadow and terror.

The Chatterer-Beast is not alone. Two other CENOBITES prowl the shadows. We can't yet see them clearly.

An ARCHWAY OF BLUE LIGHT seems to form on the far wall of the Pen. The Cenobites cease their prowling and watch...

...as Pinhead makes his entrance.

Pinhead stalks elegantly into the centre of the Pen. He glances round, registers the shattered robot, the Box, and then his eyes go unerringly to the wall-mounted camera...

INT. PAUL'S CABIN/HOLDING PEN ANNEXE, MINOS

...and he addresses Paul directly through the monitor screen.

> PINHEAD
> (on monitor)
> Merchant. I know you're watching. We'd almost given up waiting for you to play.

Corinne's face is an ashen mask of horror.

> CORINNE
> It _knows_ you?

PAUL
We've never met. But he's an old friend of the family.

Paul clicks the monitor off. He turns to Corinne.

PAUL
There it is, Corinne. The hidden agenda you kept wondering about.

CORINNE
Never mind that. *Can they get out?!*

PAUL
Two-feet thick concrete and steel.
      (beat)
And I don't know. I hope not.

A beat as they stare at each other.

PAUL
I know you need a full explanation — But I have to go and fix those alignments before the shuttle gets here.

CORINNE
Paul, the shuttle's <u>here</u>.

PAUL
Buy me time.

> CORINNE
> The government pays my wages, Paul. I have to hand the station over. I--

> PAUL
> It's a question of minutes. Vital minutes.

He stares at her, imploring. A beat.

> CORINNE
> I'll do what I can.

>> CUT TO:

EXT. MINOS, DEEP SPACE

An entry-bay door opens on one of the stone towers rising from the surface of the Minos and the Endeavour enters.

INT. ENTRY BAY, MINOS

An airlock door opens ... and we TRACK in suddenly to the SIX FIGURES that come rushing into the entry bay.

Four of them are MILITARY — uniformed, armed, and masked. The other two are civilians.

EDWARDS, bureaucratic and embittered, is a male government administrator. The other civilian is CHAMBERLAIN, a young-looking scientist.

The military is headed by CARDUCCI, a wiry and grizzled no-bullshit professional.

His tough-looking squad are ROSCOE (a powerful very tall female), RIMMER (female), and PARKER (male).

Edwards, Chamberlain, Carducci, and the soldiers (arms at the ready, scanning the area) walk into the large arrivals area. Hewn with rock, it's as much a cavern as it is a room.

(NB: PRODUCTION NOTE: This area and all the areas (mainly corridors) that are not function-specific have a half-finished laser-blasted look to them. There are grooves in the walls of the rock where corridors and walkways were blasted through. Unless specifically described otherwise, everywhere on the Minos is rock, not steel or wood or plaster.)

All of them look round at the laser-hewn space.

> EDWARDS
>
> Jesus...

> CARDUCCI
>
> How the hell do they do this?

> CHAMBERLAIN
>
> It's pretty straightforward. Tractor-

beams capture a suitably
small asteroid and then
Meta-Lasers form the
structures from the rock
itself. It's actually
cheaper than building
from scratch.

                    EDWARDS
          Cheaper until some crazy
          SOB takes it on an
          unscheduled trip.

Stacked everywhere are crates and unopened boxes. Chamberlain reads the stencil-stamp on a crate.

                    CHAMBERLAIN
          WZ-474s? They should have
          been wired in months ago.
          All this stuff...
               (glancing around)
          He's done nothing he's
          supposed to.

                    EDWARDS
          Then what has he been
          doing?

                    PARKER
               (looking at the dank rock)
          Letting this place go to
          hell.

A door opens and Corinne walks over to them. She takes in the military and then addresses Edwards.

CORINNE
Soldiers? Were you
expecting armed
resistance?

EDWARDS
Lady, when you maintain
radio silence for a full
six months, I don't know
what to expect.

CORINNE
I'm sure we can clear up
any misunderstandings.
I'm Corinne Cotton,
Administrator of the
Minos.

EDWARDS
Former administrator of
the Minos. I'm Edwards,
your successor.

Corrinne opens her mouth to speak. Edwards raises a peremptory hand to silence her.

EDWARDS
Here's what I know. The
Minos is Merchant's
baby. Six months ago, he
was ordered to hand it
back to the government.
He sent the whole crew
home except for you and
him. And then he took
the whole goddam station
out of orbit and headed
into deep space. We're

>   taking it back and we're
>   installing Dr Chamberlain
>   here as his replacement.
>   It's going to be calm.
>   It's going to be cool.
>   It's going to be clean.
>   (beat. To Carducci)
>   Fan 'em out, Dooch.

The Soldiers move out at a trot into the Station.

>   CORINNE
>   Wait! This isn't
>   necessary. We--

>   EDWARDS
>   (interrupting)
>   The only reason you're
>   not under arrest is
>   because my bleeding-
>   heart self doesn't want
>   to screw up your pension.
>   From this moment until
>   you're back on Earth, you
>   do two things: answer my
>   questions and follow my
>   orders. Got it?

Corinne nods, staring in distress at the disappearing soldiers.

INT. SATELLITE-CONTROL, UTILITIES COMPLEX, MINOS

Paul, hunched over the console, punches in co-ordinates and watches the minute movements of the satellites on the monitors. Two or three of the monitors show a graphic OVERLAY with the word LOCKED flashing. Paul's still working on the others.

Suddenly, there's a CREAK behind him. Paul spins round...

...to find himself staring directly into a gun-barrel!

Roscoe's holding the gun.

> ROSCOE
> Dr Merchant? Consider
> yourself relieved.

INT. CORRIDOR, MINOS - DAY

Rimmer and Parker walk along an oppressive, dimly lit corridor. They reach the door to Paul's cabin and the Holding Pen Annexe.

Rimmer tries the handle. Locked. She looks questioningly at Parker. He shrugs.

> PARKER
> Investigate all areas.
> That's what they said.

Rimmer leans back and delivers a shoulder-slam to the door. It opens.

> RIMMER
> So let's investigate.

She leads the way in.

INT. LOCK-UP, MINOS

Paul's face stares out from behind bars at Edwards and Carducci.

> PAUL
> You don't know what you're doing.

> EDWARDS
> Actually, we do. We're keeping you out of the goddam way while we find out what the hell you've been doing here.

> PAUL
> No! You don't understand! It's dangerous!

> CARDUCCI
> Dangerous how?

Paul looks from one to the other. Can he tell them? Would they believe him?

He has to chance it.

> PAUL
> There are demons on the ship.

Carducci bursts into LAUGHTER.

> CARDUCCI
> (to Edwards)
> Well, that solves that mystery. What went wrong

on the Minos? Dr Merchant went out of his fucking mind.

INT. PAUL'S CABIN/HOLDING PEN ANNEXE, MINOS

Parker and Rimmer make their way down through the cabin to the annexe. Parker gestures to the pen-monitor.

> PARKER
> What's this hooked up to?

Rimmer looks down the stairway to the reinforced door, then back at the monitor.

> RIMMER
> Whatever's in there, I guess.

The monitor, sensing movement, clicks on. While Rimmer makes her way down the staircase, Parker looks at the monitor. The image it shows is of the completely empty holding pen. Then a BLUE LIGHT pulses briefly over the screen.

Parker's eyes fix on the screen. Another BLUE PULSE. And another. His eyes blink and focus... and suddenly his face moves into horrified rage.

ON THE MONITOR: The holding pen is full of CHILDREN, frightened, hungry, and chained to the walls!

                    PARKER
               My God!

Fuelled by outrage, he hurtles down the stairs, levelling his weapon at the reinforced door.

BLASTS of ENERGY smash into the huge door and BLOW IT APART.

Rimmer, much nearer the door and nearly caught in the blast, throws herself aside.

                    RIMMER
               Parker, what the fuck are
               you doing?!

Parker rushes past her through the smoking ruin of the door...

INT. HOLDING PEN, MINOS (CONT.)

...and into the holding pen. At first, all he can see is shadows and light.

                    PARKER
               Where are the children?

Rimmer appears in the wrecked doorway.

                    RIMMER
               What are you talking
               about?

Parker suddenly points to the floor.

> PARKER
> What the hell's this?

Both register the SHATTERED METAL FRAGMENTS of the robot littering the floor around the Box.

> PINHEAD (O.S.)
> The remnants of a most unsatisfying victim.

Parker and Rimmer start in shock as Pinhead emerges from the shadows. Movements from all around add to the terror as the other Cenobites shuffle in the darkness.

> PARKER/RIMMER
> (simultaneous/ad-lib)
> Oh my God... What the fuck... Sweet suffering Christ... (etc)

> PINHEAD
> Still — you're here to change all that, aren't you?

A brief, imperious gesture of the demon's head...

...and a METALLIC FRAGMENT, jaggedly pointed like a badly made Shuriken, suddenly rises up from the wrecked robot spinning fast and furiously as if by magic...

...and then HURTLES ACROSS THE ROOM. Before Parker can even react, it slams into him — SLICING HIS FACE OFF.

He falls to the ground...

...and Rimmer has the sense to turn tail and run...

...but she trips on the jagged edge of the blasted door and falls to the ground.

She swings herself round and half-sits up

— just in time to see the Chatterer-Beast launch itself from the darkness and land on her, its terrible jaws slashing, snapping, and slavering.

TIME-CUT TO:

INT. PAUL'S CABIN/HOLDING PEN ANNEXE, MINOS

We are in the living quarters end of Paul's cabin. And so are Pinhead, the Beast and the Cenobites.

This is our first clear look at the other two Cenobites: One is brand-new, A SIAMESE-TWIN CENOBITE joined at the side of the head and at the lower chest and the hips.

The other is Angelique. Though her face and figure are still beautiful, she has been 'Cenobitised': Like all Cenobites, she is bald and blue-skinned and her individuality has given way to the leather-and-mutilation uniform look of Pinhead's troops.

She looks at the living quarters, at Paul's deliberate 18th century look. We see her recognise the style — and the bloodline's taste.

> ANGELIQUE
> Toymaker...

> PINHEAD
> No time for games.
> Merchant has a plan. He
> mustn't exercise it. Kill
> them all.

Pinhead, the Beast, and the Siamese-Twin move out through the room to the corridor.

Angelique lingers a moment, taking in these reminders of her past — the furnishings, the pictures, the automata.

Her hands trail over an object or two, her eyes, beneath their Cenobite coldness, helplessly nostalgic.

INT. LOCK-UP, MINOS

Edwards and Carducci are talking while Paul observes them from behind bars.

> EDWARDS
> What do you mean?

> CARDUCCI
> How much clearer can I
> be? Parker and Rimmer
> haven't radioed in.

They're missing.

Paul closes his eyes in dread.

> PAUL
> Where did you send them?

They ignore him.

> EDWARDS
> What are you saying?

> PAUL
> (louder)
> Where did you send them?!

> EDWARDS
> Quiet!

> CARDUCCI
> (to Paul)
> Your work-area.

> PAUL
> They're dead. And if you don't let me out to finish my work, we're all dead.

Carducci looks to Edwards. He nods back to Paul.

> CARDUCCI
> That's your call. I'm going to notify Roscoe and Chamberlain to proceed with caution.

Carducci exits. Edwards crosses to talk to Paul directly.

> EDWARDS
> Whatever's going on — <u>if</u> anything's going on — how the hell do I know you're not responsible?

Paul sighs. Frustrated. And guilty. He <u>is</u> responsible.

INT. LOW-LEVEL CORRIDOR, MINOS

Roscoe patrols a low-level service corridor. Dank rock. Wet floor. Dismal lighting. It's a creepy atmosphere. Shadows fool us.

We keep waiting for something to leap out at Roscoe. But nothing does. Yet. Ahead of her is an entrance door. Hefting her weapon, she goes in...

INT. FLIGHT DECK, MINOS

...and enters the Flight Deck. This is more brightly lit than the corridor, but its emptiness is still creepy. Roscoe is very much on guard and walks through cautiously, rifle cocked.

INT. SATELLITE CONTROL/UTILITIES COMPLEX, MINOS

This is the room where Corinne and Paul worked on the satellite alignments. We now see more of the room. It's the electronic heart of the Minos — a large space full of humming data banks and pulsing generators.

Wires, conduits, and fibre-optic cables run everywhere from machine to machine. Chamberlain is at a large Systems-Analysis Monitor, on which blueprint-like diagrams of the Minos flash across the screen.

> CHAMBERLAIN
> (to himself)
> He's done nothing.
> Nothing...

In the distance beyond him, unseen by him, a FIGURE moves eerily between the 'doorway' formed by two generators.

Chamberlain keeps scrolling through the data base.

> CHAMBERLAIN
> And what the hell are
> these satellites?

Suddenly, a SOUND from somewhere behind him. Chamberlain jumps in shock and swings round.

> CHAMBERLAIN
> Hello?

Nothing. Cocking his head, Chamberlain moves out into the room. He begins to walk through the machinery. Because of the stacking and positioning of the banks and the generators, the place has a maze-like feel of many intersecting small walkways.

Chamberlain makes his way down the walkways. An eerie atmosphere descends. There are SOUNDS and FLEETING SHADOWS everywhere in this place. Is something in here with him? He begins to look over his shoulder often.

His tread becomes quiet and cautious.

He turns a corner. At the end of the walkway, a vaguely human-shaped shadow. Very slowly, he moves toward it...

...to find nothing but a pile of boxes, stacked unevenly in such a way that they cast a misleading shadow.

Chamberlain exhales in relief.

                    CHAMBERLAIN
  Shit...

He turns back into the walkway he left — and is suddenly face to faces with the Siamese-Twin Coenobite.

                    CHAMBERLAIN
  What the--?!

The creature suddenly and instantly SPLITS IN TWO, its two selves springing apart and one of them sweeping past Chamberlain.

Chamberlain stands between the Twins, terror on his face.

The Twins speak, alternating words as if they are still one.

> TWIN 1/*TWIN 2*
> I *cannot* bear *to* be *apart* from *my* brother.

They raise their arms and walk toward each other...

...and RE-MERGE, their flesh stretching eagerly toward each other's, crushing and assimilating the SCREAMING Chamberlain between themselves/itself.

The Twins are Siamese again. There's nothing left of Chamberlain.

INT. LOCK-UP, MINOS

Corinne stands as close to Paul as the bars allow. Edwards is some distance away.

> PAUL
> It's what my family has lived for for two centuries. It's my destiny. My duty. To free the world from the demons my bloodline unleashed.

> CORINNE
> By building a space station?

> PAUL
> By building a trap. And

destroying them forever. But the satellites aren't ready. The Elysium Configuration can't be triggered. What I built as a <u>trap</u> has become a <u>nest</u>.

> CORINNE
> Why didn't you tell me sooner?

> PAUL
> Like I didn't seem crazy enough? Nobody need ever have known. This was meant to be a one-man operation once everything was ready. Now people are dying. I wish you hadn't stayed.

> CORINNE
> I wanted to stay.

Paul looks at Corinne as if that had never occurred to him. Her eyes are saying something they've probably been saying for months but he was too driven to notice.

She likes him. A lot.

> PAUL
> You've got to get off now. Get to a shuttle.

Corinne shakes her head.

                    CORINNE
          We've got to get you out
          of here.

INT. PAUL'S CABIN/HOLDING-PEN ANNEXE, MINOS

Carducci is at the bottom of the staircase, staring in horror at what's left of Parker and Rimmer. He flicks open a tiny intercom.

                    CARDUCCI
          Roscoe? Where are you?

                    ROSCOE
              (on intercom)
          Flight deck.

                    CARDUCCI
          Can't raise Chamberlain.
          Don't know what the
          fuck's going on. But
          shoot first. You copy?

                    ROSCOE
          Check.

Carducci pockets the intercom and makes his way up the stairs.

ANGLE ON The living quarters part of the room. We hear the sound of Carducci climbing the stairs — as does the Angelique Cenobite who is still in the room.

She crosses to closet. Its door is a full-length mirror. She swings it open. The inside door is also fully mirrored. She pauses for a moment to look at her reflection on the inner door. The reflection is of her former self, in all its human beauty.

The Angelique Cenobite STEPS THROUGH THE MIRROR — coming out the other side as her human self.

ANGLE ON Carducci as he reaches the top of the stairs and moves into the cabin...

...to see Angelique sitting on the bed, a look of terror on her face.

>ANGELIQUE
> Help me. Please help me...

Carducci scans the room quickly, on guard.

> CARDUCCI
> What's happened? Are they here?

Angelique stands up. Carducci crosses to her. Doing a perfect imitation of a pre-feminist damsel-in-distress, Angelique throws her arms round this big strong man and presses her poor helpless self to him for protection.

They are standing in front of the still-open mirror-door.

> ANGELIQUE
> No. Not now. But they're everywhere. I'm so

afraid...

Carducci can't help it. He's a professional. But there's a beautiful woman pressing herself to him. He relaxes his body and puts his arms round her...

>   CARDUCCI
> Hey, it's okay.
> Everything's okay.

...and Angelique suddenly pulls them both backwards. She slips from his arms but keeps tight hold of one of his hands and steps back through the mirror, emerging on the other side as her Cenobite self!

Carducci is halfway through the mirror. It seems while she has hold of his hand, he too can pass magically through as if the mirror were liquid...

Unfortunately, she lets go.

And Carducci is suddenly SCREAMING IN AGONY. The mirror is once-again-solid — and he's on either side of it!

Angelique swings the mirror shut — and one half of the perfectly-bisected Carducci slides smoothly and bloodily down the mirrored glass.

INT. FLIGHT DECK, MINOS

Roscoe is still moving through the flight deck. She's alone... until a door at the far end opens and Pinhead walks in.

Roscoe's jaw drops. But training tells. She assumes a firing position and shouts a warning.

> ROSCOE
> What the fuck planet are you from? Hold it! Right now!

Pinhead doesn't stop. Nor does he speed up. He just keeps walking. Confident. Inexorable.

> ROSCOE
> Had your chance.

She pulls her trigger. An ENERGY BLAST slams into Pinhead...

...and does nothing. Doesn't even make him break his stride. Nor does the second.

> ROSCOE
> Mother of Christ.

Roscoe stares at the Demon. She's a huge powerful woman, so she's not exactly afraid. But she's not exactly stupid either and staying here would plainly be the act of an idiot.

She turns and runs, slamming through a door...

INT. FLIGHT-DECK CORRIDOR, MINOS (CONT.)

...into the corridor. Still running, she scans the area for somewhere to hide. Her eyes go up to the ceiling...

...and a grill to an air-duct. It is too high to reach but a utility pipe which runs parallel to it is a vital few inches lower.

Roscoe leaps, catches the pipe with both hands, swings herself up, and kicks the grill clear, throwing her body in after it.

INT. AIR-DUCT, MINOS (CONT.)

Roscoe grabs at the grill, shoves it back into place, and presses her body back into shadow while leaning her head just enough to see through the cross-hatched metal of the grill.

ROSCOE'S POV DOWN THROUGH GRILL: Nothing. Nothing. Nothing... and then Pinhead walks into view.

Roscoe holds her breath.

Pinhead keeps walking. Not looking up. He's nearly past the grill...

And then he stops. His head tilts up a little, as if sensing something...

...and then he moves on out of view.

Roscoe breathes gain.

                    ROSCOE
               (mouthing it)
         Alright

She waits a second to be sure and turns in the air-duct...

...to see the Chatter-Beast twenty yards from her!

                    ROSCOE
         Oh fuck!!

She doesn't even have time to bring her rifle round in the cramped space. The Beast comes rushing along the duct. In two seconds, it's there, its awful mouth opening wide...

                                   CUT TO:

INT. LOCK-UP, MINOS

Corinne is over with Edwards. Paul is still in the cell.

                    EDWARDS
         Give me a break.

                    CORINNE
         I'm completely serious.
         He has to be let out.
         He's the only chance we
         have. I've <u>seen</u> them.

Edwards stares at her.

The seriousness of her tone almost holds his disbelief at bay. Then rationalism reasserts itself.

> EDWARDS
> Let him out? I should put you in there with him! People might be dying out there!

> CORINNE
> That wouldn't have happened if the government had left him alone.

> EDWARDS
> Well, excuse me. Obviously, it's _our_ fault.

Corinne sighs. Enough argument.

> CORINNE
> We're letting him out.

> EDWARDS
> _We're_ not doing anything. _I'm_ the administrator and I--

Corinne half-turns, as if she can't listen anymore — and then swings back and DECKS Edwards with a powerful right hook.

> CORINNE
> Former administrator. I'm

                    your successor.

She moves to the desk and hits some buttons. The barred door of Paul's cell flies open. Paul rushes over to her as Edwards rises groggily to his feet.

                    PAUL
          I don't know how far
          things have gone. You'll
          have to help me.
               (looks to Edwards)
          Both of you.

                                        TIME-CUT TO:

INT. CORRIDOR, MINOS

Paul, Corinne, and Edwards run along a corridor. They reach a three-way crossroads and stop.

                    PAUL
          You both know what to do.
          You both know where to
          go.

                    EDWARDS
          This is insane!

                    PAUL
          Yes, it is. You need to
          accept that if you want
          to come through this.
          You seem to be a man of
          reason. Don't be.

Shaking his head, Edwards nevertheless takes off down one of the corridors. Paul turns to Corinne.

                    PAUL
          You've been brave. Stay
          brave. Stay alive.

Corinne looks as if she wants to say something. She just nods and turns to go.

                    PAUL
          Corinne?

                    CORINNE
          Yes?

                    PAUL
          My... My life was planned
          from the moment I was
          born. From before I was
          born. I had no time for
          anything but the destiny
          I was given.

He pauses, looks deep in her eyes.

                    PAUL
          I wish my life could've
          been different.

A beat.

They reach out, and touch each other's hand briefly. And then they're away down different corridors.

INT. LOW-LEVEL CORRIDOR, MINOS

The Cenobites, Pinhead leading, move along in implacable rhythym while the Chatterer-Beast scurries and slides, weaving around and about the others.

As the monsters pass, the space behind them DARKENS as if they are dragging endless night in their wake.

INT. FLIGHT-DECK, MINOS

Paul rushes in to the flight-deck and runs over to the master console. His expert fingers fly over various keys and buttons. Monitors show the exterior images of the satellites — three of which still flash the LOCKED signal. He looks at the others anxiously.

INT. CORRIDOR CROSSROADS, MINOS

A set of double doors is smashed open from the other side and Pinhead stalks into an area where two corridors meet. His monstrous troop flows in behind him.

As before, BLACKNESS follows them, all light vanishing as they pass.

>   ANGELIQUE
> If Merchant is finally
> playing again, the stakes
> must be high.

> PINHEAD
>
> His gamble is trusting other players.

Pinhead looks down at the Chatterer-Beast. He points an imperious arm down one of the corridors.

> PINHEAD
>
> Fetch!

The Beast takes off at incredible speed. Angelique and the Siamese-Twin go after it. Pinhead goes the other way.

INT. FLIGHT-DECK, MINOS

Paul holds a slim black object in his hand. Some kind of remote-control. He points it at various console switches and it glows red as if reading information from each one.

He looks overhead. Two angle-poises point down to where he's standing behind the console. He hits a button and they both shine a combining light on him.

He looks back at the monitors. All the satellites are not yet locked. He looks into the room as if awaiting the inevitable arrival of his enemy.

INT. HOLDING PEN ANNEXE, MINOS

Edwards walks into the annexe. He stares

in shock at the blasted reinforced-door and the bloodstains and bones that are all that remains of Rimmer and walks through...

INT. HOLDING PEN, MINOS

...into the Pen. Suppressing a shudder at the CORPSE of Parker, he scans the area...

...and sees the Box. He picks it up, turns to leave...

...and sees Angelique in the blasted doorway!

>   EDWARDS
> Oh, no.

Angelique walks into the Pen — and the Siamese-Twin follows.

Edwards looks from them down to the Box in his hand.

>   EDWARDS
> He... He told me what to
> do with this.

Angelique's face creases in contemplation as she looks at the man. She thinks she's got his number.

>   ANGELIQUE
> Please. Go ahead. If you
> think it will do you any
> good.

Edwards runs his fingers listlessly over the Box. He presses at it a few times as if looking for hidden buttons. Nothing. His arms drop hopelessly, and he starts to sob.

> EDWARDS
> It's... a box. It's just a fucking box.

He lifts it and flings it half-heartedly at Angelique.

Her hand rises and catches it expertly.

> ANGELIQUE
> Thank God for men of reason.
> (to the Siamese-Twin)
> Finish it.

She turns and walks away, not even watching as Edwards falls to his knees sobbing in fear.

The Siamese-Twin towers over him and SPLITS.

> TWIN 1/*TWIN 2*
> I *cannot* bear to be apart from my Brother...

CUT TO:

INT. FLIGHT-DECK, MINOS

The only sounds in the flight-deck are

the hum of the mechanisms and the sound of Paul's tense breathing.

And then there's another sound.

The sound of demonic feet approaching.

Paul looks up from the console. Angelique has entered, holding the Box. Their eyes lock, each recognising and acknowledging their bizarre history.

> ANGELIQUE
> Building bigger toys than ever.
>
> PAUL
> The Minos is no toy. It's--
>
> ANGELIQUE
> I know what it is. Don't use it. I saw your room. The past means as much to you as it means to me. We can reclaim it. Together.

Paul looks at her. For a second, the same magic that worked on John works on him and he has a FLASH-IMAGE of her human self in 18th century costume. Beautiful. Alluring.

He blinks it away. His face sets grimly.

> PAUL
> Not this time, Princess.

Disappointed rage crosses her face. Before she can answer, they are no longer alone.

Pinhead and the Siamese-Twin have entered.

The DARKNESS comes with Pinhead and then changes into BLUE LIGHT diffusing in from various angles as if the doors to Hell are open.

Simultaneously, HOWLING WINDS begin to roar through the room, necessitating raised voices.

Pinhead looks at Paul standing behind the console in the light from the two overhead angle-poises.

> PINHEAD
> How the centuries pass.
> I've thought often, down
> those long days, of
> the pleasures we have
> prepared for you.

> PAUL
> Pleasures?

> PINHEAD
> In a manner of speaking.
> Your ancestors have been
> there before you. The
> Labyrinth still rings
> with the echoes of their
> agony — Lullabyes for the
> Children of the Worm.

Paul looks at the monitors. Two more satellites are showing the LOCKED signal.

> CUT TO:

INT. SATELLITE-CONTOL, MINOS

Corinne feverishly types in co-ordinates and watches the monitors click one by one into the LOCKED position.

Finally, the words ALL SATELLITES ALIGNED show on the master monitor.

Corinne sits back and lets out a long slow sigh.

>   CORINNE
>   Alright, girl. You passed
>   the science exam. Now
>   let's see how you do at
>   track.

She exits the room...

INT. CORRIDOR, MINOS (CONT.)

...and out into a corridor. And starts running.

Fast.

INT. FLIGHT-DECK, MINOS

Paul's eyes register the ALL SATELLITES ALIGNED signal.

He shows no relief or excitement. Good poker player.

PAUL
It's over now. It ends with me.

PINHEAD
I think not. Your bloodline may end but the game goes on forever. Four hundred years your family has played. A long time? No. The blink of a suppurating eye to He Who Dwells In The Deep.

PAUL
The game may go on forever, but you won't be there to play it.

ANGELIQUE
Fly us back to your world, toymaker. No end of games there.

PAUL
I'm afraid I can't do that.

ANGELIQUE
Want to play here? Well, you won't be playing with this.

She holds out the Box.

Pinhead smiles.

Paul doesn't.

                    PINHEAD
            Good. The woman?

                    ANGELIQUE
            A gift to our chattering
            friend. You know how fond
            he is of female meat.

INT. CORRIDOR, MINOS

Corinne reaches a T-junction. She turns left into...

INT. LONG CORRIDOR, MINOS (CONT.)

...the longest corridor we've seen yet. It stretches at least a hundred yards on either side of the T-junction.

Just before renewing her run, Corinne looks down the other stretch.

A hundred yards of emptiness...

But not for long. Appearing suddenly at the far end comes the Chatterer-Beast, careering towards her down the corridor.

                    CORINNE
            Oh my God.

Corinne wastes a precious second staring at it, her jaw open in horrified shock. Then she turns and runs for her life.

And the beast runs for it too.

It's nightmare-fast, seeming to gain thirty yards for every ten that Corinne covers. Within a few seconds of the chase stating, it's almost halved the distance between them.

Not wanting to — and hardly able to afford to — Corinne nevertheless can't resist looking back over her shoulder.

She registers how, as the creature passes, the walls behind it become a nightmare of darkness and despair.

> CORINNE
> (to herself)
> Run. Run!!

And she does. Panting, sweating, heart pounding, she runs.

The demon pursues her vigorously and tirelessly, gaining yard by yard as it speeds furiously down the corridor.

Gasping with exertion, Corrinne stares desperately ahead of her at the door she's heading to. It seems closer...

> CORRINNE
> Come on! Come on!

She redoubles her effort...

...and suddenly she trips, cartwheeling to the floor.

As if sensing her sudden weakness, the

monster behind her HOWLS in infernal delight and streaks forward even faster.

Corrinne scrambles to her feet, runs on, and suddenly she's there.

She bursts through the door...

INT. ENTRY BAY/ESCAPE VEHICLE PAD, MINOS (CONT.)

...and tumbles into the entry bay.

Immediately ahead of her a small single-person egg-shaped ESCAPE POD sits on a pad beyond the open station-side door of an airlock.

Corinne rushes to the pod, slams her hand on the release catch of the door, and clambers in.

INSIDE POD —

It ain't built for luxury; There's a contoured body panel into which Corinne stands, a control panel in front of her, a round window and that's it.

On the control panel is a sticker marked AIRLOCK REMOTE and beneath it two toggle switches, one marked INTERNAL which is clicked to the OPEN position and one marked EXTERNAL which is clicked to CLOSED.

Corinne flicks the INTERNAL to CLOSED.

IN THE ENTRY BAY —

The airlock behind the pod begins to close...

But simultaneously the doors to the bay burst open and the Chatterer-Beast leaps into the room.

INSIDE POD —

Corinne looks at the slowly closing airlock door and at the far from slow Monster rushing toward her.

> CORINNE
> No. No...

The door's not going to close in time. She's fucked. She groans... and then thinks of something.
She slams forward the switch that says BRAKE and then hits the one that says IGNITION.

IN THE ENTRY BAY —

A massive THRUST OF JET-PROPELLED FLAME slams out of the back of the stationary pod, blasting the Beast back across the room.

The jet-flame is cut in time to allow the airlock door to close without being melted.

IN THE AIRLOCK —

The outer airlock door slides open.

The ignition starts again...

EXT. MINOS, DEEP SPACE - (CONT.)

A beat of stillness...

...and then the egg-shaped Pod comes spinning wildly toward camera.

Corinne is safe.

INT. FLIGHT-DECK, MINOS

Paul isn't. CLOSE on his face, stiff with tension.

PULL BACK to reveal why —

The viciously barbed tips of several of Hell's Hooked Chains are hovering inches from his face and body, taut and swaying like steel King Cobras waiting to strike.

A cruel smile illuminates Pinhead's face as he stares at Paul.

Paul looks at another monitor providing entry-bay date. The words POD-LAUNCH are flashing. He signs in relief — and then looks up at Pinhead and Angelique.

> PAUL
> It didn't get her. She's free. She's safe.

> PINHEAD
> May that prove a comfort
> to you when the maggots
> are eating your eyes.
> From the inside.

Paul's eyes suddenly become fixed and cold. Like gunfighters in a spaghetti western, Paul and Pinhead stare at each other.

> PAUL
> Let's play.

His fingers dive at the buttons...

...but Pinhead's so much faster — and the hooked chains jet forward viciously to pierce Paul's body and face...

...and Paul just WINKS OUT of existence, disappearing down to a white dot like a turned-off TV.

Or a cancelled hologram.

> ANGELIQUE
> What?

Paul steps out from another part of the room entirely.

He has the remote-control in his hand.

> PAUL
> Hologram. All done with
> mirrors. Like this.

His finger hits a button on the remote...

CUT TO:

EXT. MINOS, DEEP SPACE

The Minos floats against the star-studded blackness.

Suddenly, VAST BEAMS OF LIGHT burst from all six satellites! Like Lemarchand's design, like John's miniature version, the beams meet and EXPLODE into a HUGE CORUSCATING CAT'S CRADLE completely encircling the Minos, dwarfing even that vast structure in an awesome and dazzling light show.

INT. FLIGHT-DECK, MINOS

Pinhead, Angelique, and the Siamese-twin all stagger as if suddenly weakened dreadfully. The Box falls to the ground from Angelique's slackened grasp.

>   PINHEAD
>   NOOOO!!!

He raises his hands as if to summon chains or other tools...

...and nothing happens.

EXT. MINOS, DEEP SPACE

The show gets even bigger. As if reality can't cope with the massive Cat's-Cradle, a HUGE STORM IN SPACE erupts around the

Minos, a maelstrom of roiling gases and impossible lightning.

The Cat's-Cradle of light suddenly sends out a LIGHT BEAM into the space behind it.

The Beam smashes into a mass of bubbling gaseous matter, WHITES-OUT briefly...

...and is replaced by an area of intense blackness, a corona of gaseous matter swirling about its edges, defining its position.

The nebulous swirl seems to be disappearing constantly into the unrelieved blackness of the centre.

It is as if the Cat's-Cradle has sundered reality, has created an astronomical anomaly.

A place where matter disappears.

INT. FLIGHT-DECK, MINOS

Pinhead looks over at Paul, horror-struck

> PINHEAD
> What have you done?! What is it?!

> PAUL
> Endgame, demon.

Angelique screams.

EXT. DEEP SPACE

The Minos suddenly judders within the Cat's-cradle and begins to hurtle toward its furthest point — the swirling black reality-warp.

INT. FLIGHT DECK, MINOS

Pinhead ROARS at Paul — and from his open mouth a CHAIN flies toward Paul...

...and hooks into his chest. Paul grunts in pain, but grasps the chain, yanks it, and pulls Pinhead toward him. The two enemies grasp each other's arms, wrestling and fighting, somehow keeping their balance in the wildly careering deck.

As Angelique and the Siamese-Twin are knocked helpless to the floor, Pinhead and Paul scream to be heard in the cacophony.

> PINHEAD
> In Hell, I'll teach every
> one of your nerve-endings
> to scream separately!

> PAUL
> You still don't get it?
> It's over! Finally,
> irrevocably over!!

EXT. DEEP SPACE

The Minos is now careering toward the

reality-warp at an incredibly increased speed.

And suddenly, within the Cat's-Cradle and almost within the irresistible blackness, the Minos begins to break apart, unable to withstand the terrible pressures!

INT. FLIGHT DECK, MINOS

A SMASH-CUT to Paul and Pinhead as, all around them, the deck disintegrates. A frozen second for Paul's last line...

>   PAUL
>   Welcome to Oblivion.

EXT. DEEP SPACE

...and then, just as it disappears into the gaping maw of the warp, the Minos comes apart completely in a massive explosion.

THROUGH THE WARP/PSYCHEDELIC SPACE (BLUE SCREEN)

The MONTAGE BACKGROUND is a whirling insanity of images: spiralling patterns; the birth of planets; exploding supernovae; volcanic eruptions; the works.

Asteroid DEBRIS spins wildly in the foreground, piece after piece being whirled away until finally we see the Box left alone above the background — the perspectives of which all sell the idea that it is constantly falling even though its image size remains constant.

Slowly, the camera TRACKS IN on the Box until the black circle that dominates one of its faces FILLS THE SCREEN.

And then, without quite realising when it changed, we realise we are tracking OUT, not in...

...moving through an EXTREME CLOSE UP of the Box and continuing out...

INT. LEMARCHAND'S WORKROOM NEARLY MIDNIGHT

...and we see that the Box is resting on the hand of Phillip Lemarchand in his workshop in 18th century France.

The door opens and Genevieve enters in her nightdress.

> GENEVIEVE
> Is it done?

> LEMARCHAND
> Done!

CUT TO BLACK

RUN END CREDITS

About the Author

Author photo: Keith Payne

Peter Atkins helped mind-fuck a generation by writing three Hellraiser movies in the 80s and 90s. He has spent the subsequent decades disappointing his original fan-base by writing quirky little ghost stories in which, for the most part, nobody gets skinned alive. He can't apologize enough. He is the author of the novels *Morningstar, Big Thunder*, and *Moontown*, and his short story collection, *Rumors of the Marvelous*, was a finalist for the British Fantasy Award.

He tweets as @limeybastard55

Printed in Great Britain
by Amazon